common
paths

To Joe & René

Love Patty Bultman

Psalm 119:105

common paths

a novel

Patty Bultman

TATE PUBLISHING
AND ENTERPRISES, LLC

Published by Tate Publishing & Enterprises, LLC
127 E. Trade Center Terrace | Mustang, Oklahoma 73064 USA
1.888.361.9473 | www.tatepublishing.com

Tate Publishing is committed to excellence in the publishing industry. The company reflects the philosophy established by the founders, based on Psalm 68:11,
"The Lord gave the word and great was the company of those who published it."

Book design copyright © 2015 by Tate Publishing, LLC. All rights reserved.
Cover design by Gian Philipp Rufin
Interior design by Jimmy Sevilleno

Published in the United States of America

ISBN: 978-1-63418-043-6
1. Fiction / Christian / General
2. Fiction / Contemporary Women
15.01.20

In memory of Dominic Cole Esarey
I promise to always remember you and smile.

Dominic's poem

As we look to the horizon
Everything begins to blur
We wipe the tears from our eyes
As those feelings begin to stir

We did not know the torment
That you'd been going through
We only kept on seeing
What you really wanted us to

We saw your outward smile
But not your inner pain
We never really dreamt
That you'd never smile again

Forgive us if we failed to see
What we could have done to aid
Or if we failed to understand
How much you were afraid

We pray your mental anguish
Will now forever cease
And that your deep anxieties
Can be replaced by peace

We will try to remember
The good times, not the bad
Remember all your smiles
And not when you were sad

So when we think about your life
We won't dwell upon its close
We'll remember all the good times
And forget about life's blows

Our lives have been made better
Because you have been there
Now we're left with your memories
And your laughter hanging in the air

Gone, but Never Forgotten
Kyrie Esarey

In all your ways acknowledge Him,
and He will make your paths straight.

—Proverbs 3:6

chapter one

The sun peeked over the horizon like a child playing peek-a-boo in the heart of the Bible belt. The sky is a vast canvas splattered with pink and orange hues. The sunrise was just a glimpse of God's splendor and creativity. Abigail watched as the morning sun spilled light upon a new day in the rural Kansas town she called home. God was telling her good morning.

She sat curled up on the antique porch swing, a hot cup of tea warming her hands. It was her favorite spot to spend quiet time with the Lord. She loved sitting on the porch watching the first light of day burst from the horizon. She took the quilt draped over the back of the swing and covered her legs. The slight chill in the air signaled the beginning of fall.

The red geraniums that once graced the front steps of the old Victorian house had been replaced with purple and gold pansies. Abigail would wait a few more weeks before adding pumpkins to the autumn décor.

She took a sip of the warm tea. Her mind was racing with questions. There was so much she wanted to share with the Lord, and she longed to hear from him. She anticipated the joy and peace that would overcome her when she laid her concerns at the foot of the cross.

Her heart was burdened with memories from her past. Thoughts of one particular day consumed her mind. It was the day that had changed her life forever. It had also been the moment God placed a dream in her heart.

It had been a scorching August day. The flowers had withered in the brutal heat. The grass had crunched beneath her feet, brown and desperate for rain. After a month in the mental hospital, she felt withered and dry like the foliage around her. She was finally free, but as the nurse closed the door behind her, she realized she was free in more ways than one.

She had spent years imprisoned emotionally and spiritually, and for the first time, she finally felt her spirit being renewed. She was no longer a patient, locked behind closed doors, and while that made her happy, it had also terrified her.

Before coming to the mental hospital, Abigail's life had been about one thing—herself. She had caused her loved ones so much pain and heartache. Would they ever forgive her for all she had done?

Trying to end her life had been the most selfish thing she had ever done. Although she regretted her attempt, fear haunted her like a ghost.

"I'm so sorry, Lord," Abigail whispered. "Why would you waste a minute of your precious time on me?"

The Holy Spirit stirred in her soul like the breeze rustling the nearby trees. The leaves were beginning to turn beautiful hues of red and gold. She took a long sip of tea as she watched the leaves slowly float to the ground.

Abigail talked to God as if he were a close friend, sitting beside her on the wicker swing.

"It's because of your great love for me that you've never turned your back on me and that you never will."

Abigail was captivated by God's promises to her.

Her past was full of disappointment, failure, and sin, but God had never given up on her. Despite three divorces, an abortion, and running from God, he had pursued her with intensity.

He blessed her when she didn't deserve it. In the midst of so much pain, she had given birth to a precious son, landed a job that brought her peace, and gained many wonderful friends.

God had given her the gift of making things beautiful. Interior design brought her peace when nothing else could. God promised to give her a future full of hope.

"I don't want to be the wretch I once was," Abigail prayed. "Thank you for saving me from myself. There's nothing I can do to make you love me more and nothing I can do to make you love me less, and that truth has set me free."

It wasn't long after Abigail had been released from the mental hospital that God began to reveal his plan for her life. She smiled as she thought back to the moment she first heard him whisper his plan to her heart.

It wasn't an audible voice, but deep within her spirit, she heard God say, "There will be a Peace House."

At the time, she had had no idea what God was asking of her. She tucked his instructions away in the back of her mind, trusting he would reveal more of his plan in his time.

She had spent the past eighteen years praying for God to guide her and show her what the Peace House was supposed to be.

She had thought he had given her the Peace House when she married Adam and they moved into their first home. Or maybe it had been when God blessed them with the quaint house next door, a safe haven for women and children in need of love and a glimpse of their Heavenly Father.

As more women and children began to show up on her doorstep, Abigail questioned God. "What do you want me to do? You have to show me what you mean when you say 'Peace House.'"

But he just kept whispering, "Be still and know that I am God."

As Abigail waited on the Lord to guide her, she continued to be obedient and minister to the many women and children God placed in her life. She shared her love for God's Word with them, and through the Scriptures, they learned about his love, mercy, and grace.

As they began to hunger and thirst for more of the Word, Abigail began holding weekly Bible studies in her home. The more time she spent ministering to the women, the more God confirmed that she was to expand her ministry and open a home for the women and children God kept putting in her path. Working with the young women reminded Abigail of who she once was and the faithfulness of God. If he could redeem her life, she knew he could redeem every woman who walked through her door.

On more than one occasion, houses became available for the Peace House, but each time, the offer fell through.

Had Abigail heard God wrong?

For years, she rented multiple houses around town for the girls she ministered to. She believed the girls deserved a roof over their heads and a warm bed. Those basic necessities were critical if she wanted to guide them toward their Savior.

God had graciously allowed Abigail to witness many women accepting the precious gift he offered.

If her ministry only touched *one*, then she had succeeded. Her job was to make sure the women knew where they would spend eternity. It was about discipleship and putting love into action.

She believed Isaiah 55:11, which promised that "God's Word would not return void."

Abigail sat her teacup on a small table next to the porch swing. She smiled as she thought how far God had brought her. He had used each season of her life to prepare her for this moment.

It was finally time to watch her dream—God's dream—of a Peace House unfold.

As she continued soaking up the morning sun, Abigail thought back on the past six months. It seemed like yesterday that the unlikely trio had united over a box filled with books, money, and letters.

Ruthie, Abigail, and Mimsey were nothing alike, but a unique friendship had developed.

As the three joined forces to find the owner of the mysterious box, it became clear that common threads, like hope, faith, and grace, tied them together.

Their search led them to Mrs. White, an elderly woman bound to a wheelchair. Abigail was drawn to Mrs. White. The wrinkles on her face vanished with each smile, and there was a sweet fragrance about her. It reminded Abigail of fresh-baked cookies.

Abigail was intrigued by more than her smile and joy-filled eyes. Like herself, Mrs. White had a desire to help women and children in need. She had always dreamed of opening a retreat center.

"Lord, you brought Mrs. White into my life to help fulfill this crazy dream you've placed on my heart," Abigail whispered. "You never cease to amaze me."

Mrs. White had used the box and its contents to lead the trio to her so that she could share her God-sized dream.

"My wish, and what I believe is God's plan, is for you to open a retreat center for women," Mrs. White told them on that unforgettable Spring day.

Abigail was in awe of how the Lord had put her and Mrs. White, a woman who shared her passion and dreams on a common path.

Mrs. White had surprised the trio when she told them she wanted to bestow a house and the financial resources to open the retreat center.

Although there was a house, and money available to start the ministry, Abigail still wasn't sure how the details would fall into place.

Mrs. White's health was failing, and Abigail wasn't sure if she'd live to see her dream fulfilled.

"I am asking you to show me the dream that you gave Mrs. White for the Peace House," Abigail prayed. "I don't want to get in the way of exactly what you want. I know Mrs. White wants to go home to be with you, but could she stay until she sees the dream she so desires?"

Abigail trusted God's promise. She believed God would give Mrs. White the desires of her heart.

"We just want to love people like you do. We want your compassion, your eyes. Break our hearts for what breaks yours," she prayed. "Guide our every thought, word, and deed. Thank you for listening. In Jesus's name I pray these things and give you all the glory and praise. Amen."

During the months that followed Mrs. White's announcement, more and more women began gathering at Abigail's house for Bible study. The women represented many churches in town, but despite their differences in denomination, they were learning that the love of Jesus was what truly mattered.

Abigail sensed God preparing hearts for the Peace House. God had a specific calling for each of their lives. God was calling each of them to action. The roles they would play would look different. God would use their pasts—the good and bad—their skills and their talents for his kingdom. God had gathered the perfect team, and the women didn't even know it yet.

Abigail was disappointed that Mrs. White couldn't join them today. She was about to tell the Bible study girls the wonderful news.

"Ladies, I have something very exciting to share with you," Abigail said.

The chatter in the room ceased as the ladies directed their attention to Abigail. Ruthie and Mimsey stood on either side of her, beaming with excitement.

"Thanks to our dear friend Mrs. White, Peace House Ministries now has a home," Abigail said.

Cheers rang out. A frenzy of conversation buzzed around the room.

The women had prayed for this moment for so long and were full of questions.

"I know we're all excited, but I think the best thing we can do is pray and ask God to lead us as we set out on this new adventure," Abigail said. "Leta, would you please pray for us?"

Abigail and the women joined hands and bowed their heads as Leta began to pray.

> Lord, you have graciously given us a house to be the home of Peace House Ministries. We know you have a plan for it, and we want your will to be done and not ours. This house will only be used for your glory and for your purposes. As women are invited to study and retreat here, we ask for your mighty Holy Spirit to fill this home, every nook and cranny, from the foundation in the basement to the tip top of the roof. We want your Holy Spirit to dwell in the Peace House. Lord, let no evil or undesirable spirit enter into this home. Lord, we give you all that will be studied here, videos that share your Word and about how to make your Word come alive in our lives. We pray every book will be used to grow us spiritually and draw us closer to you.
>
> Let the joy and peace that comes from you be felt as every soul enters in. Lord, as we plan every event, we ask you to guide us. We believe each retreat is planned for a group of women that you desire to help, heal, and encourage. Please use us to do exactly what you want, the way you want it, and may the results be absolutely what you desire.

Please guide each lady to the Peace House, for only you know when she will be ready for healing or when she is in need of encouragement. We know each women needs to feel your love in an amazing way in this home and take that love with her into her home as she leaves. Lord, as you bring ladies to the Peace House, we know many things will need to be in place. I ask you to provide women who can minister and share their stories with those attending.

Lord, you use broken women who have accepted your healing to perform these tasks, so others have hope in the midst of their seemingly hopeless situations. Lord, I thank you for healing those who will be used in this Peace House to help others. Lord, bless those who will cook and clean and do the laundry, the jobs that may seem meaningless. I pray those women know how important they are to this ministry. Every job is absolutely necessary to make the retreats stress-free and *peaceful*. I pray everyone who steps into the Peace House will feel your presence. I pray that so many prayers are spoken here that it will also be known as the House of Prayer or the Miracle House. Lord, I thank you for the opportunity and the privilege to pray, and I thank you in advance for how you will answer these prayers. Lord, we love you and thank you so very much for all you do and all you plan to do here at the Peace House. Lord, I thank you for the words in John 14:27, "Peace I leave with you, My Peace I

give you." Thank you for your peace. It cannot come
from anywhere else. I pray in the precious name of
Jesus. Amen.

After the prayer, the women sat in silence. Abigail wiped
tears from her eyes.

"Thank you so much for that beautiful prayer," Abigail
said. "She had been feeling overwhelmed, thinking of all
that needed to be done to make the Peace House ready for
women's retreats, but the prayer had brought peace to her
anxious heart.

After the time of prayer and celebration, the women
began to leave one by one, each of them offering to use their
unique God-given gifts to help prepare the Peace House.

God had called Abigail to love women and lead them to
him, and he had provided a place for that to happen. His
timing was perfect, and she had to remind herself that he
would make a way. There was no reason to become anxious.
God had it under control.

Later that night as Abigail climbed into bed, the anxiety
was replaced with excitement. She began to dream about
what the Peace House would look like.

As a decorator, she had visions of the beautiful colors
she would use to paint the walls—earthy greens, deep reds
and beautiful golden colors. She wanted inviting furniture

where the women could curl up, get comfortable, and stay a while.

She wanted to decorate the living area with sparrows, a reminder that God cares for the little things; no sparrow falls to the ground without God knowing. The large room was adorned with a fireplace and lots of tall Victorian windows that allowed natural light to pour in. Abigail had received a large photograph of a sparrow sitting on a barbed wire fence as a gift. The portrait would be the perfect addition to the room. It had the words from the hymn "For his eye is on the sparrow" written on it.

I sing because I'm happy.
I sing because I'm free.

And of course, there had to be sweets. Abigail could almost taste the sugary sweetness of the cupcakes, cheesecake, and Bundt cakes she would serve the women staying at the Peace House. Abigail loved baking for others.

As Abigail led a group of young ladies through the book *Healing for Damaged Emotions* Workbook by David Seamands and Beth Funk, she was reminded how God had used the book to heal her own broken places.

The girls were embracing God's love and forgiveness. That evening they had witnessed God's miraculous healing. One of the girls had come to class with terrible neck pain, unable to turn her head. As she read during the study, the pain in her neck completely went away, and she was able to move it freely. They had witnessed healing before their eyes.

"I knew I didn't need to go to the chiropractor," the young girl exclaimed. "I just needed to pray, and I did. Look what God did!"

Abigail witnessed everyone's faith grow that evening. She was excited to see what God had in store for each of them. Once they finished the study, they would celebrate with a retreat at the Peace House.

Abigail felt pressure to make the house perfect for the first retreat which was only a few months away, and for these women who had worked so hard to overcome the challenges they faced. So much still had to be done, and she wasn't sure how it would happen in such a short period of time. Thankfully, God did.

For I am convinced that neither death nor life, neither angels nor demons, neither the present nor the future, nor any powers, neither height nor depth, nor anything else in all creation, will be able to separate us from the love of God that is in Christ Jesus our Lord.

—Romans 8:38–39

chapter two

Despite the mistakes of her past, God had blessed Abigail. He had showered mercy and grace upon her when what she really deserved was death. She loved what she had learned about grace and mercy. The difference is that grace is getting what you do not deserve and mercy is not getting what you do deserve.

Her husband Adam was proof of God's goodness. After spending years in unhealthy relationships, God had brought the man he had always intended for her to love.

They had worked hard, praying and reading the Bible together daily, to build their marriage on the unwavering foundation of Christ. As they obeyed the Lord, his blessings continued to be apparent in their lives. They became parents, and then grandparents, when their son Mark learned he had a nine-year-old son.

His son, Nick, was living with his maternal grandparents and wanted to find his biological father. His grandmother agreed and began searching for Mark. She soon discovered Mark lived only a few miles away from them.

It wasn't long before a DNA test was ordered and the results proved Mark was Nick's father.

Abigail and Adam were thrilled to know they had a grandson, but fear had consumed Mark. He didn't know how he would explain the surprising news to his wife, Amanda.

They had been trying to start a family for so long and had recently been told by doctors that it would be impossible for Amanda to carry a child. Adoption looked like their only option if they wanted to be parents.

Mark's news was going to come as a shock to Amanda as it did to him, but Abigail had prayed they would love this child unconditionally.

Mark yearned to give Nick a normal childhood. As a teenager, Nick's mom had never been able to give him a life of stability and eventually left him in the care of his grandparents.

Abigail prayed for Mark and Amanda, that meeting Nick for the first time would be absolutely wonderful, a God appointment. She prayed the presence of God would be there and his will would be done.

Mark, Amanda, Abigail, and Adam and the entire family welcomed Nick with open arms and a desire to make up for the nine years they had missed. He was a precious boy, handsome, tall with dark hair and a contagious smile. He had an incredible love for books and read at a higher level than most kids his age. He could spend hours with his nose stuck in a book. He loved to make people laugh; he was a boy excited with life.

Abigail was in awe of God's plan for her son and grandson. After years of yearning to find his dad, Nick finally had. Mark had the desire to be a parent, and God gave him Nick. Nick also got a whole family to love him with that wonderful unconditional love.

Abigail remembered the mixture of excitement and nerves she felt the first time Nick stayed with her. She wanted to make him feel special the way any grandmother would. She decided to prepare his favorite lunch, which was to her own relief grilled cheese sandwiches. It was a simple lunch; surely she wouldn't mess it up.

So she buttered the bread, unwrapped a slice of cheese, and listened as the sandwich sizzled when she placed it in the frying pan. Nick sat watching her, a look of curiosity on his face. She scooped the sandwich up with a spatula and placed it on a plate. She set it in front of Nick, but he didn't make a sudden move to gobble it up. Abigail hoped Nick didn't notice the look of disappointment on her face. What had she done wrong? She had buttered the bread and added the right amount of cheese. She even cut it into triangles, the way Nick's daddy had liked it as a child.

"Is something wrong with your sandwich?" Abigail asked.

"I don't really like burnt grilled cheese," Nick said.

"Oh," Abigail said. "Did I not make it correctly? How do you do it?"

"You just get two pieces of bread, put a slice of cheese in between, and put it in the microwave for fifteen seconds," Nick said.

Abigail laughed as she picked up the plate containing the burnt grilled cheese.

"Obviously your grandma needs some practice making grilled cheese," Abigail said with a smile. "Let's make a new sandwich together and I bet it will be just the way you like it."

The grilled cheese saga had been a turning point for Abigail and her grandson. She explained to Nick that he could always talk to her about anything, even her inability to make grilled cheese sandwiches.

"Just because you do something one way doesn't mean others do it the same way," Abigail said. "We have to tell each other if something isn't going how we think it should."

It was the beginning of many sweet conversations between Nick and Grandma Abigail. Abigail found herself asking her grandson how he had done things in the past. He shared his way of doing things and then asked Abigail to explain hers.

Their conversations progressed from grilled cheese sandwiches to bigger things, things about God and the Bible, heaven and creation, all were so very interesting to him. She loved it as Nick began to share his heart with Abigail.

"I'm so glad I found my dad and that I'm a part of this family," he said.

Abigail smiled and thanked God for the miracle sitting beside her.

Mark and his family lived only a few blocks from Adam and Abigail. Nick would ride his bike over and spend the days baking and playing basketball with Abigail. Some days they would take trips to the skate park, and Abigail cherished the moments she spent watching Nick do amazing tricks on his skateboard.

One day, during their time together, Nick confided in Abigail. "Grandma, I wish I had a brother or a sister," he said.

"If God has a sibling in his plan, it will happen exactly when it's supposed to," Abigail said. "But for now, we are all so happy to have you as part of our family. You have so many family members who love you so much."

"I know, Grandma."

Mark and Amanda knew how much Nick wanted a sibling. They wanted to give him a brother or a sister but weren't sure how they could after receiving the news from their doctor.

After a lot of research, they discovered a doctor in a foreign country who believed they could have a biological child. For the first time in a long time, they were filled with hope at the thought of having another child and giving Nick a sibling.

They began raising money for the trip overseas and the medical expenses. Abigail and her friends prayed fervently. She knew the situation could either cause great joy or more pain if it didn't work out.

Once again, God was faithful. He heard and answered the many prayers, and nine months later Abigail was blessed with another grandson.

Mark and Amanda finally had the baby they had dreamed of, and Nick was excited to finally be a big brother to Bradley.

Being a grandmother filled Abigail with a joy like nothing she had ever experienced. Her joy overflowing, she often thought of how God knew the very special bond he would create between a grandma and grandchild. Her cup was running over with joy—the boys, the Peace House, and her design business. Her plate was full, but she cherished every busy detail.

The Peace House was coming along slowly. Repairs were being made to the house before remodeling could begin. Abigail, Ruthie, Mimsey, and Mrs. White took advantage of the time they had and gathered the items they would need to furnish the house. People were donating things left and right. It was awesome to see how the Lord was providing for the dream he had placed in their hearts.

Abigail believed God had big plans for the new long-awaited Peace House. There would be retreats, Bible studies, and life skills classes. Every aspect of the adventure was causing excitement to bubble up inside of the foursome. They met often to discuss their ideas and make plans for the first retreat, which would be for the girls who were currently in the Bible study called *Healing for Damaged Emotions*.

After they completed the book and twelve weeks of studies, they were lavished with love for a weekend at the Peace House retreat. It was a great incentive to stick with the in-depth study.

Abigail had witnessed amazing healing throughout the weeks of the study and God was being glorified through the lives of the girls. The Lord wasn't just working in the girls' lives, but in their children's lives as well.

Recently, Casey and her sons Alex and Jaden were blessed with a rent house. The day the family of three moved into their new home, Abigail and Adam realized the boys still didn't have a bed to sleep in.

The five of them knelt down and prayed for bunk beds.

After the prayer, Abigail's phone rang and she answered it.

"Hi, Pastor Ben," she said.

"Hi, Abigail, checking to see if you need any help moving Casey and her boys into their house," he said.

"We've got them moved in, but we are trusting that the Lord will provide bunk beds for the boys," Abigail explained.

"Well, it looks like your prayer has been answered," the Pastor said. "It just so happens that I have a set of bunk beds that you are welcome to have."

Abigail was astonished by God's goodness.

"Adam and I can head over right now to get them," she said. "Thank you so much!"

As Abigail hung up the phone and shared what had happened, she witnessed a miracle.

"God was listening!" Alex exclaimed.

Tears fell down Casey's cheeks as she hugged her sons.

In that moment, Abigail knew God had used a set of bunk beds to remind this family of three of how much they were loved.

Look to the Lord and His strengths;
 seek His face always.

—Psalm 105:4

chapter three

Abigail couldn't get the phrase out of her mind.

"What does love require of me today?"

She carried a warm cup of tea, her Bible, and a journal and went out onto the porch. She sat on the porch swing and whispered, "Lord, what are you trying to tell me?"

She opened her Bible and the pages fell to the book of Micah. As she began reading, a verse jumped off the page.

> What does the Lord require of you? To act justly and to love mercy and to walk humbly with your God.

God was pulling Abigail outside of her comfort zone. She had been traveling and speaking to different groups about the Peace House. She shared how God had asked her to help those in need by giving them a hand up, instead of a handout.

She loved meeting new women from all walks of life, but she wasn't particularly a fan of speaking. She became a bundle of nerves before each event and had to rely on God to guide her and give her the words to say. She was scheduled to speak the following day, and the butterflies were already dancing in her stomach.

As she let God's word sink into her spirit, he reassured her of the calling he had placed on her life. An interaction between God and Moses suddenly came to Abigail's mind. She flipped the pages of her Bible to Exodus and read the story where God revealed his plan for Moses to bring the Israelites out of Egypt.

> Moses said to the Lord, "O Lord, I have never been eloquent, neither in the past nor since you have spoken to your servant. I am slow of speech and tongue."

Like Abigail, Moses had felt inadequate to fulfill God's plan for his life. But God had reassured him, and he was doing the same for Abigail.

Now go. I will help you speak and will teach you what to say.

Abigail had asked Ruthie to attend the event with her. She shared a special bond with Ruthie. Upon moving to the small Bible-belt town, Ruthie had been the first person outside of church comfortable enough to talk about Jesus.

Ruthie glowed with the love of Jesus more than anyone Abigail had ever seen. Their friendship became deeper and more rooted in Christ every time they were together.

Abigail had invited Ruthie to join her because she loved praying for the women after Abigail shared her testimony.

That morning when they arrived at the church, the presence of the Holy Spirit overwhelmed them.

Abigail noticed most of the women in attendance were African-American. She suddenly felt self-conscious of her blonde hair and fair skin.

Now go. I will help you speak and will teach you what to say.

Abigail and Ruthie took their seats as the music started. She immediately noticed the genuine worship happening around her. She loved praising the Lord with these women, even if she couldn't keep a beat. Women from the local rape crisis center and homeless shelter were there. Abigail prayed that her testimony, which was full of hope and forgiveness, would be exactly what the ladies needed to hear.

Abigail stood in front of the women, opened her Bible, and began.

"I recently heard it takes pain to bring about change. Think of the pain Jesus endured for our sins. I share my story today because I promised God I would be obedient. I pray it gives you hope.

"I have had three failed marriages, been stuck in an abusive relationship, attempted to take my own life, took the life of my innocent unborn child, and was rejected by my church. I have suffered so much pain and anguish, but because of Christ I have hope.

"Jeremiah 29:11–14 says, 'For I know the plans I have for you,' declares the Lord, 'plans to prosper you and not to harm you, plans to give you hope and a future. Then you will call on me and come and pray to me, and I will listen to you. You will seek me and find me when you seek me with all your heart. I will be found by you,' declares the Lord, 'and will bring you back from captivity. I will gather you from all the nations and places where I have banished you,' declares the Lord, 'and will bring you back to the place from which I carried you into exile.'

"Believe God's promises. Believe he restores what's been broken. I'm living proof he redeems. I believe he can redeem your broken places too."

Abigail looked at each of the women and saw the promise their lives held. Many of them wiped tears from their eyes. God had fulfilled his promise. He had given her the words to speak, but not without tears. Abigail had yet to share her testimony, a story filled with horrible choices and deep sin, without becoming emotional.

The best part about giving her testimony was sharing how God had redeemed her life.

The women burst into applause and many wiped tears from their eyes. Abigail knew they sensed God's love and forgiveness, his peace and joy, and most of all, his hope.

"Just remember, God will not give up on you," she said. "If you would like someone to pray with you, we would be honored to do that now."

Dozens of women made their way to the front. Abigail and Ruthie took their hands and listened to the heavy burdens weighing on their hearts. They prayed over each woman and were filled with joy, humbled to be a part of God's plan for healing and restoration in their lives.

As the time of prayer came to a close, the women were invited to go downstairs for lunch. As they filled their plates with sandwiches, salads, and desserts, two police officers walked into the room.

"Excuse me," one of the officers said. "Is Abigail Kurtain here?"

A sick feeling settled in the pit of Abigail's stomach. The women watched intently as she walked toward the officer.

"Mrs. Kurtain, would you mind coming upstairs with us?" the officer asked.

Abigail, Ruthie, and two ladies from the church followed the officers up the stairs.

"Is everything okay?" Abigail asked as they walked toward a more private room. The officers didn't answer her, and the sick feeling became more intense.

"Please have a seat," the officer said as he ushered the women into the room.

"Mrs. Kurtain, you need to call Pastor Robert as soon as possible," the second officer said. "He's been trying to get in touch with you and has left a dozen messages."

"I had my phone turned off while I was speaking," Abigail said. She dug through her purse to find her cell phone. Her heart pounded in her chest. She looked at the officers, her eyes begging them to tell her what was going on.

"You just need to call Pastor Robert," the first officer said. "We will stay here until you have talked to him."

"Is my husband okay?" Abigail asked. Tears began to sting her eyes. Fear paralyzed her.

The officers didn't say anything as she fumbled with her phone and dialed the number.

Pastor Robert answered on the first ring. "Abigail, I wish I didn't have to tell you this news," he said.

Abigail was shaking. The tears fell fast.

"*What was happening?*"

"Your grandson, Nick, is dead, Abigail. He took his own life."

Abigail tried to process what she had just heard. How could her fourteen-year-old grandson be dead? Her mind was spinning. She tried to stand up, but her legs were weak, unable to hold her weight. One of the officers grabbed her and guided her back to the chair.

She suddenly realized Pastor Robert was still on the phone.

"Abigail, have someone drive you home as soon as possible," he said.

The officers carried a limp and shocked Abigail to the car as the ladies from the event began praying over her.

Pastor Robert was a dear friend, but not Abigail's pastor. He led the church across the street from Mark and Amanda's house. When he saw the police cars at their home, he had gone over to help. He learned that Nick had shot himself. Adam was there but was unable to reach Abigail.

Ruthie drove as fast as she could, but it was the longest thirty-five miles of Abigail's life. The pain was unbearable.

When they arrived at Mark and Amanda's house, it looked like a crime scene. Adam and the police were doing all they could to get Mark and Amanda out of the house. Neighbors had heard horrific screams coming from the house as Mark and Amanda found their son's body lying in a pool of blood.

In the midst of her anguish, Abigail felt relief when she learned that Bradley had been with Amanda's mother.

As they stood amidst the chaos, Abigail looked at Ruthie and wondered if she was having flashbacks of her daughter's murder. She had witnessed every horrific detail, and now her dear friend was experiencing something no mother or grandmother should ever experience.

Ruthie didn't leave Abigail's side. Had it not been for her, Abigail wouldn't have made it through the days that followed her grandson's death. Abigail's pastor was another source of strength. The two of them were the hands and feet of Jesus.

God showed his love through each visitor, each meal prepared, every flower, and each word of encouragement and sympathy.

Abigail and Adam clung to one another and to God. Their grief ran deep, and their hearts were burdened for their son who had just experienced something no parent should ever have to.

One visitor had told Abigail, "The only thing worse than losing a child is losing a grandchild and having to watch your child mourn the loss of their child. It should never have to be."

Those words rang in Abigail's ears for many nights. Nick had touched so many lives. The pain of his death was taking its toll on so many. His family and friends were heartbroken.

The funeral was a celebration of Nick's life. Abigail wanted to shout, "Suicide is a permanent solution to a temporary problem. I never want any of you to ever feel hopeless!"

At that moment God's word comforted her: "For I am convinced that neither death nor life, neither angels nor demons, neither the present nor the future, nor any powers, neither height nor depth, nor anything else in all creation, will be able to separate us from the love of God that is in Christ Jesus our Lord" (Romans 8:38–39).

The reason for Nick's suicide was unknown. How she wished she had known the burden he was trying to carry on his own, the pain he was feeling. What had caused him to make such a drastic, life-altering decision?

She racked her brain trying to think of reasons why Nick would feel hopeless that day. But she knew it didn't do any good tormenting herself with things she would probably never understand this side of heaven.

She found comfort in the pastor's words during the funeral.

"Nick was on God's team," he said. "He loved God and his Word. He got the call for the plan and heard it wrong. He made the wrong play, but it didn't get him kicked off the team. He is now with Jesus in heaven."

The days and weeks following the funeral were filled with writing thank-you cards and tying up loose ends. At times, the pain was so fierce she couldn't breathe. She cried enough tears to fill an ocean, but standing beside her were her precious broken family and her dear friends, Ruthie, Mimsey, and Mrs. White.

Abigail wondered if God was punishing her for taking the life of her unborn child, or her own suicide attempt, but God quickly reminded her that he doesn't work that way.

She prayed: *Dear Lord, our hearts are broken by this horrific tragedy; help us to feel your love and give us more faith.*

The more she sought after God, the more Abigail realized she had to live. She had to decide if this tragedy would make her bitter or better. Everything in her wanted to cling to bitterness, but she knew God wanted her to let go and trust him, she didn't need to understand to trust.

She knew there would be good days and bad days, but Christ would be the solid rock she would stand on. It would just take facing each day one at a time.

"For I know the plans I have for you," declares the Lord. "Plans to prosper you and not to harm you, plans to give you hope and a future. Then you will call upon me and come and pray to me, and I will listen to you. You will seek me and find me when you seek me with all your heart."

—Jeremiah 29:11–13

chapter four

Abigail was tempted to cancel all her ministry events. The death of her grandson had paralyzed her, but God kept whispering to her soul, "Give me your pain, and I will use it for my glory."

A week after the memorial service, despite her attempts to cancel a speaking event that had been on her calendar for months, God nudged her to go.

Mimsey offered to drive Abigail to the out-of-town event. Abigail asked her to have a speech prepared in case she didn't have the courage to speak in front of the ladies so soon after the loss of Nick. Abigail knew Mimsey could cover for her if she needed to. She had watched God do amazing work in her friend's life.

Abigail smiled as she remembered the day Mimsey Magness came to her door a few short years ago. She was dressed in flattering designer jeans and a cashmere sweater. She was always wearing the latest fashions and had cute accessories to match. Abigail's life hadn't been the same since Mimsey became a part of it. She definitely added spunk and she thanked God for her precious friend.

Mimsey had been so hesitant to talk about God when Abigail first met her. Abigail believed that with each treasure they opened from the box, Mimsey began to open up a little more. It was because of the box and its contents that Mimsey had accepted Christ as her Savior.

The morning of the event was hurried. Abigail had many things to finish up before she and Mimsey headed out of town. She prepared for the weekly Bible study that would be held at her house the following day.

The ladies were studying the book of James, and Abigail was trying to memorize the first chapter. She was struggling, wrestling with God, about how she could possibly consider the tragedy that had occurred to her family pure joy. But she was supposed to. God's word said, "Consider it pure joy, my brothers and sisters, whenever you face trials of many kinds, because you know that the testing of your faith produces perseverance. Let perseverance finish its work so that you may be mature and complete, not lacking anything."

Abigail would choose to persevere starting today, as she would speak for the first time since Nick's death.

She heard a knock on the door, followed by Mimsey's bubbly hello. "Hey, you ready to go?" Mimsey asked.

"I'm so nervous," Abigail said as she gave Mimsey a hug.

"You'll do fine. I've been praying for you all morning."

"I was just going over my memorization for Bible study. God keeps reminding me I have to persevere."

"That's right," Mimsey said. "What's the verse about pressing on for the prize?"

"Philippians 3:14," Abigail said. " I press on toward the goal to win the prize for which God has called me heavenward in Christ Jesus."

"Well, let's press on!" Mimsey said as she dragged Abigail toward the door.

Abigail laughed. She could always count on Mimsey to lift her spirits.

"Mimsey, are we going the right way?" Abigail asked.

"This is the way I usually take," Mimsey said. "We have plenty of time to get there."

As they reached the turn in the highway, they noticed heavy traffic and road construction. As they crept along, they noticed a woman carrying heavy bags and walking along the side of the road.

"Did you see that woman?" Abigail asked.

"Yes, but she's going the opposite way," Mimsey said.

"I know, but I know we must stop to check on her."

Mimsey pulled the car onto the side of the road and waited for traffic to clear before she turned around and headed in the direction they had just come.

Abigail rolled her window down as they pulled up beside the woman.

"Where are you headed?" Abigail asked.

"I'm on my way to a shelter," the woman said, not slowing down to look at Abigail or Mimsey.

"We are on our way to a women's event at a nearby church," Abigail said. "We would be happy to take you to the shelter after the event."

Mimsey looked at Abigail, concern spread across her face. Obviously, she'd never picked up a hitchhiker, Abigail thought to herself. She just thought she was driving me to a speaking event and praying me through it.

"Are you sure you don't mind?" the woman asked.

"Not at all," Abigail said. "Hop on in."

The woman opened the car door and threw her heavy bags on the floorboard. She climbed into the back seat and settled in for the ride.

She looked rough and tough, about forty-five years old. She was stocky, about five-foot-four with flame-red hair. She was wearing jeans and sweatshirt, definitely not the attire for a women's salad supper at a local church.

"My name is Mae," she said.

"It's nice to meet you, Mae. I'm Abigail, and this is my friend, Mimsey."

As they drove toward the church, Mae shared her story. She had recently been released from prison. She had come to Kansas to attend her brother's funeral and to visit her sister. Her brother-in-law didn't want a visitor any longer, so she had no other choice but to go to the shelter. The only way to get somewhere safe was to walk the twenty-six miles to the shelter.

About the time Mae had finished sharing her story, Abigail received a text message from a friend in California. It read, "Praying that you will be able to share what God wants you to during the event today."

Her friend had included the song "I Will Trust You" by Chris Lizotte.

"This song is meant for you right now," the text continued.

Abigail found the song on her phone, and the three women listened to the words as they drove. It was a beautiful song about trusting God, even in the midst of sorrow.

The three women loved the truth portrayed through the song lyrics.

"I've never heard such a powerful song before," Mae said.

As they arrived in Greensburg, Abigail pointed out devastation left from a tornado that had ripped through the community five years earlier. The town was holding an anniversary event called Tragedy to Triumph that weekend.

When they arrived at the church, they were ushered inside and warmly welcomed by a group of warm-welcoming women. Abigail introduced Mimsey and Mae, and they found their seats at the table reserved for them.

The old Abigail would have made sure the church women knew that Mae was a hitchhiker who needed to be shown the love of Jesus. She was glad she was no longer *that* person. It was so much better to just call Mae her new friend. The women treated Mae with kindness, and she fit right in, even though she wasn't exactly dressed for a salad supper.

During dinner, a lady sitting at the table began talking about the wonderful day she had spent with her grandson.

Abigail froze. Reality hit her like a ton of bricks. She would never get to spend another day with Nick. She leaned over and whispered in Mimsey's ear. "I can't do this. I'm not ready." She willed herself not to cry. "Please excuse me," Abigail said. "I need to stop by the ladies room before I speak."

Abigail hurried down the hall and locked herself in the bathroom.

"I can't do this, God. How can I share the miracles you have done for me? I want to be obedient, but this pain is suffocating me!"

Abigail let the hot tears fall freely.

Then she heard it. His still small voice.

I will do it for you. Trust me. You stand there, and I will speak through you.

Abigail wiped the tears from her face, took a deep breath, and walked back to her table.

Abigail took another deep breath and looked out over the crowded room. It was a much larger group than she had anticipated. The event coordinator had to keep adding tables and chairs to accommodate all the women.

She opened her notes and her Bible. She opened her mouth, and God filled it. Before she knew it, she was on her last page of notes. Had she really spoken an hour like they had requested? Every eye was fixed on her, and most of them were moist with tears.

She had even shared the gut-wrenching story of Nick's suicide.

She stepped away from the podium and went back to her seat next to Mimsey.

"You just delivered the best speech of your life," Mimsey said.

Abigail knew it wasn't her, but God had once again fulfilled his promise.

Abigail, Mimsey, and Mae loaded the car and prepared to head to the nearby shelter. Before they were even out of the parking lot, Abigail heard soft cries coming from the back seat. She turned to see Mae crying.

"Mae, what's wrong?" Abigail asked. She turned toward her new friend and placed her hand on her leg.

"When you spoke about your abortion, I knew God was speaking to me," Mae said. "I went through so much counseling and rehabilitation in prison, but I never shared my darkest secret."

Abigail had a feeling she knew what the dark secret was. She had spent years trying to hide hers.

"Would you like to tell us?" Abigail asked.

Mimsey pulled the car to the side of the road and put it in park.

"This is a safe place," Mimsey said. "You can talk to us."

"Twenty-five years ago, I had an abortion," Mae said. "Tonight God showed me that my abortion was the root of all the sin I've committed. It's the reason for all the pain I have suffered. When I was released from prison, I didn't really feel free. Tonight, I finally do."

"Praise Jesus," Abigail exclaimed. "May Mimsey and I pray for you?"

"Please," Mae said, wiping away the tears that continued to fall.

Abigail took Mimsey's and Mae's hands, and there in the car on the side of the road they prayed that God would forgive Mae and set her free from the bondage of her past sins.

"Lord, we pray that the mission the devil has had over Mae will be cancelled by the power of the blood of Jesus," Abigail prayed. "In your most precious name we pray. Amen."

"Amen," Mimsey said.

"Two angels picked me up off the side of the road today," Mae said. "You didn't just give me a ride. You gave me the freedom that I have longed to have for so many years."

Mimsey pulled the car onto the road, and they made their way to the nearby shelter. When they arrived, they hugged Mae and promised to pray for her. They would never forget the God appointment that had occurred that day.

As Mimsey and Abigail headed home, they were in awe of God's wonder. They prayed and thanked him for fulfilling his plans for them that day.

"To think I might have missed this if I had cancelled the event," Abigail said. "It feels so good to be in his will. Only by the grace and mercy of the Almighty could we even be a tiny part of his enormous plan."

"I will shout a big Amen to that," Mimsey said with a smile and a giggle. "But please don't tell my husband I picked up a hitchhiker."

Direct me in the path of your commands,
for there I find delight. Turn my heart toward
your statutes and not toward selfish gain. Turn my
eyes away from worthless things: preserve my life
according to your Word.

—Psalm 119:35–37

chapter five

Although she was still grieving for the unexpected death of her grandson, Abigail knew she had to get back to work. God had things for her to do. She would choose to get better, not bitter.

She chose to trust God and put her faith totally in him, even though she didn't understand why he had allowed such a tragic thing to happen.

The tragedy had made Abigail realize that her focus needed to be on her family, especially her son, daughter-in-law, and grandson. She had to cover them in prayer. The evil one would be waiting to attack in their time of grief. His goal was to kill, steal, and destroy.

She had talked to Adam, and they had agreed that Abigail would begin watching Bradley three days a week so that his mommy and daddy could return to work. They had to try and find normalcy, whatever normal was.

The family moved into the little red house next to Abigail, which had been one of the first Peace Houses. Adam and Abigail loved their son and his family with the love of Jesus, and comforted them. They trusted the Lord to heal their broken hearts.

Abigail decided to close her interior design shop. Although she would miss it, she knew God was directing her down a different path. She would continue to counsel those in need on the days she wasn't watching Bradley. She would also spend all her free time praying for the restoration process of their lives and for the new Peace House.

Abigail knew God's timing was perfect. God had given her the promise of the Peace House eighteen years earlier when she was released from the mental hospital. She had spent years praying for God to show her exactly what he had in mind for Peace House Ministries.

She knew he wanted the Peace House to be a place for women who needed to be restored and renewed by God's Holy Spirit. Only God knew Abigail would also be restored and renewed by the Holy Spirit in the Peace House.

The new Peace House was amazing, and there was no doubt that God had a plan for it. Deep down, she was thankful God hadn't given her the final home for the ministry sooner.

For so long, she had thought the Peace House would be a place where young mothers and their children would live while being taught life skills and covered in God's love. But God had made it clear that it would be a retreat center, just like Mrs. White had told her.

The house and the plan for it was more than Abigail could have dreamed, just like Ephesians 3:20–21 said,

> Now to him who is able to do immeasurably more than we ask or imagine, according to his power that is at work within us, to him be the glory in the church and in Christ Jesus throughout all generations, forever and ever! Amen.

The outside of the house was adorned with wide steps and beautiful iron handrails. The spacious porch, with its soft green wicker furniture was sure to be a popular spot among the women. The red pillows were so inviting, bright, and cheerful. Abigail wasn't sure how anyone could pass by without wanting to sit a while and reflect on the goodness of God. Red geraniums, lots of them, lined the porch steps. The details of the house were God's doing. He is the one who fills our spaces with peace, if we just ask. And the ladies had asked. They had invited God to be the king of their home and they wanted it to glorify him. It was obvious he had heard their requests.

The cherry red front door beckoned and welcomed guests to step inside. With a push of the doorbell, church bells chimed to announce a guest, ready to be greeted with his love.

Hidden behind the door were beautiful hardwood floors, recently refinished. The paintable wallpaper, a deep chocolate cherry, was a warm welcome.

In the dining room stood the massive table that had been donated to the Peace House. Abigail had painted it the color of artichokes and stroked the names of Jesus all across the top.

Prince of Peace.

Savior.

King.

I Am.

Truth.

Redeemer.

The Rock.

The fabric seats of the old chairs needed a facelift. Abigail chose a beautiful black fabric with hints of reds, gold and greens that swirled into a beautiful pattern. The colors pulled the room together.

Abigail's sister, an artist, had painted a huge canvas of red geraniums, which hung over the antique buffet. The buffet had belonged to Adam's great-great-grandmother. The ladies from Bible study had donated their beautiful crystal and elegant serving pieces, which Abigail used as accent pieces in the room. She wanted every dinner served in the room to be exquisite.

During all her travels, she had stumbled upon many memorable places and eaten many unforgettable meals. She wanted to recreate some of those experiences for the women who would walk through the doors of the Peace House.

The powder room was one of her favorite rooms in the house. The first time she saw it, she knew she wanted to decorate it in a nontraditional way. She wanted to put scripture all over the walls but felt it would be disrespectful to use pages from the Bible. She had no idea how she would cover the walls with scripture until the idea came to her one morning during her devotion. She was reading *Jesus Calling*. The leather-bound book was full of God's Word, in large print, and it always spoke directly to her. The scriptures written out on the bottom of each page gave her an idea. She could try to apply the beautiful words from God to the walls of the powder room, but how?

She had done a technique with tissue paper, so maybe something similar would work. She decided to give it a try. As she shared God's love with each of the girls who showed up at her door, she often invited them to help her with the powder room project. Tearing the pages from the book seemed wrong, but it was going to be a great reconstruction of the book.

As the house transformed into a peaceful retreat center before her eyes, Abigail's desire for a place where God's presence was obvious, only intensified. She wanted the women who entered the house to sit in God's presence and soak up his love.

She wanted just the right furniture. Every color had to be perfect. Every detail had to be inviting, drawing them closer to Jesus. It wasn't long before God began tugging on the hearts of others to donate their beautiful furniture. Each piece was beautiful. The shades and colors were exactly as Abigail had imagined. The Lord, Great Designer, had blessed the Peace House with the perfect pieces.

Abigail dreamed of a kitchen filled with the sweet aroma of cupcakes, Bundt cakes, and cheesecake.

There was just one problem. The kitchen was tiny.

Since the formal dining room would be used, Abigail decided to remove the table in the kitchen to make room for a workstation and baking center. She wasn't sure how she would afford the kitchen remodel, but she trusted God to provide.

Soon financial donations began to appear, some were earmarked for renovation projects. If Abigail searched for the best deal, the donations would be more than enough to cover the kitchen remodel. God was providing.

Her first challenge was to find someone to replace the countertops for a reasonable price. The bids she had received seemed extremely high.

She hoped Mimsey could help her. Mimsey had replaced the countertops in her house, and the old ones were collecting dust in her garage. Her husband had wanted to haul them away, but Mimsey hadn't let him. She hoped they might be needed one day. Abigail hoped the contractor would be able to cut and repair the old countertops to fit in the kitchen of the Peace House.

As Abigail tore out the old countertops, she discovered a treasure. A nail that was hammered into the chimney had been covered by the countertops, and hanging on the nail was a beautiful string of pearls on a gold chain.

There was no way to tell how many years the treasure had been hidden there. The pearls reminded her of the ones Mrs. White had placed in the box that Ruthie had found. She was amazed again when she took them to a jeweler who confirmed they were real and valuable.

The day the workers came to install the countertops, Abigail and Mimsey prayed they would fit perfectly. As the work crew moved the countertops into the kitchen, they overheard one of them say they could be problematic.

"Lord, please don't let this be problematic, please let the countertops fit," Abigail prayed. "This will save us so much money."

The workers were able to install the countertops. They were a perfect fit. And she was thrilled!

There was a piece of unused countertop remaining that Abigail decided would be perfect to place on top of a workbench she had discovered in the basement. After a paint job and a bit of checkered duct tape to trim the edges, it would be perfect. It would be used as the baking prep area. It would be a place for the girls to gather to learn cooking skills.

The kitchen was coming along. The old carpet had been replaced with recycled rubber tiles, and the walls had been painted Granny Smith Apple green. The kitchen was accented in black and white, checks, and polka dots. To add a festive touch, cherries adorned many of the finishing touches.

Abigail, Mimsey, and Mrs. White began making a wish list for the Peace House kitchen. They needed to fill the cabinets with kitchen necessities. Everything from potholders to pans, spoons to spatulas, and towels to Tupperware. A red KitchenAid mixer was Abigail's special wish.

The following Sunday, during church, Mimsey announced an open house for the Peace House. She asked the congregation to consider buying kitchen items to fill the cabinets.

After the service, a man approached her and said his mother had passed away. His father was living in a nursing home.

"I have a kitchen full, and no one to use the things there," he said. "I would love to donate the items to the Peace House."

The items donated were perfect, everything on the list they had made was checked off, even beautiful serving dishes. His mother had been a bridge player, and she loved to entertain. God was in the business of details. The only thing on the list they did not receive was the red mixer. Abigail smiled thinking about the provision of her Lord.

Okay, she thought, *maybe a red mixer is not important. It's a wish, not a necessity.*

Abigail could see God's hand in every detail of the renovation. He continued to surprise them with the ways he provided.

One day Ruthie drove down the alley looking for items that could be used for the Peace House. (She still loved finding things that others didn't want and turning them into treasures.) She came across an auction that was wrapping up.

She saw workers loading books—hundred and hundreds of them—along with an old typewriter, and desk. As Ruthie looked closer at the books being loaded onto the trailer, she realized they were all Bibles and Bible study books.

What if they were planning to throw the Bibles away?

Ruthie worked up the courage to ask what they were planning to do with the trailer full of books.

"We're taking them to the dump," one of the workers said. "Nobody wanted these old things."

"Can I take them?" Ruthie asked.

The worker had looked at her funny but agreed to give the books to her.

Ruthie called Abigail and Adam, and they hauled the trailer full of books to the Peace House.

They spent an entire Sunday sorting through the books, Bibles, and study guides and organizing the library. As Mimsey and Abigail placed books on the shelves, they were amazed once again at God's provision.

The typewriter would add so much character to the Peace House. Abigail decided it would be displayed in the prayer room on the old metal desk. As they were cleaning it, they discovered letters and money tucked in a small drawer.

Was she really experiencing something so similar to what she had already experienced? The box Ruthie had found was full of letters, books, and money. Now they were staring at a room full of books and a drawer full of letters and money.

God was showing off again and confirming that this was all a part of his plan!

Abigail knew Mrs. White would be arriving soon. She decided to grab her shopping list and head to the store to get the items she needed for the open house. She wanted Mrs. White to have some time alone at the Peace House. She knew Mrs. White was seeking God's will for the Peace House and would spend her time there in prayer.

The house had yet to open to the public, and many were itching to see the transformation. The open house would be the perfect time for everyone to see the new house and God's abundant blessings. Abigail prayed God would receive all the glory and visitors would see the eternal plan behind the Peace House.

The four women would share what God had been doing in the ministry and put to rest the rumors about what it was not. The Peace House would not be a place for homeless people to live. It would be a retreat center where God could minister to those in need. The Peace House would not provide long-term housing for women and children. The women would love the lost and teach the saved.

The neighbors were in a bit of panic because they didn't want homeless people hanging around their property and cars blocking their driveways. Abigail knew God's plan wasn't to make the neighbors fearful.

She knew it was their job to make them feel safe. The neighbors needed to be in agreement with the Peace House and all that it stood for. Abigail wanted the neighbors to feel his peace and love.

God was giving them a chance to reach beyond the walls of the Peace House. The open house would be the time to share their mission with the interested people of the community. They came—over two hundred people walked through the house and heard of the mission God had given Abigail all those years ago. The ladies from the Bible studies helped to welcome and give tours of the house. Gifts of congratulations and best wishes were sent to the house. Beautiful flowers and gorgeous green plants and a "God wink," as Abi called it—the bright red mixer she dreamed of having—were given by those who shared in the love of God's plan.

Let no one ever come to you
without leaving better and happier.

—Mother Teresa

chapter six

As the renovation process neared completion, Abigail knew it was time to start hosting Bible studies.

Fear began to creep in.

"Lord, you've given us this beautiful place for your love to shine. Don't let me get ahead of you. Don't ever let my will get in the way of your will. Give me your eyes, your compassion, and your plan for this place. In the Mighty and Powerful name of Jesus, I pray."

Faith soon replaced fear.

Abigail loved Bible study days. She was always excited to study God's word and praise and worship him with a group of women who loved him and were devoted to him.

God had given Abigail an idea that she thought would bless many others, especially the girls and their children from Tuesday night Bible study.

Abigail felt God tell her to bake forty dozen cupcakes. She knew it would be doable with help. She had purchased one hundred beautiful cupcake boxes several years before, and they would be perfect for packaging the sweet confections.

On Sunday, after church, Ashley, one of the Bible study girls, along with three little girls—Salena, twelve, Aracely, eleven, and Angelica, nine, set out to help Abigail with the baking.

The group took a trip to the grocery store and bought twenty cake mixes, five dozen eggs, and all the other ingredients they would need for the cupcakes and frosting.

Ashley was great at math; she helped figure out exactly how much of each ingredient would be needed to bake and decorate forty dozen cupcakes.

The grocery store was full of hustle and bustle like it normally was. People waved and smiled at the group. Abigail and the girls returned each smile and shared details of their cupcake project.

"It would be such a nice surprise to receive a box of cupcakes," the clerk said as she scanned the eggs and boxes of cake mix.

Once they returned to the Peace House, they piled the items they would need on the counter. Mixing bowls, spoons, measuring cups, the cake mixes, and other ingredients.

They mixed and poured and ended up baking 224 white cupcakes. After they cooled, the girls topped each cupcake with fluffy, sweet frosting. They had so much fun baking, laughing, and dancing to music in the kitchen.

The next step was to decorate the cupcake boxes. The girls wrote, "Jesus Loves You" and "Merry Christmas" on each box.

They boxed up a few dozen cupcakes and were ready to make their first deliveries. They decided to deliver the cupcakes wherever God led them. Their first stop was to a neighbor.

The neighbor opened the door and was greeted by three little smiles and voices proclaiming Merry Christmas.

"What are these for?" the neighbor asked.

"For you," the girls replied. "We just wanted you to know that Jesus loves you."

The neighbor smiled as she took the box from the girls. "Thank you," she said.

The next delivery went to the woman who had purchased the red mixer for the Peace House kitchen. The cupcakes were the first product of that wonderful gift! She was delighted to find the girls on her doorstep holding a dozen cupcakes just for her.

Abigail's heart was full of joy. She was having such a great time blessing others with the simple, sweet gift of a cupcake.

Tuesday morning came, and the ladies gathered for Bible study. They were going to bake more cupcakes after the study. Abigail was excited to spend the day at Peace House, make cupcakes, and visit with the girls.

"Who wants to stay and help bake cupcakes after we finish the study today?" Abigail asked.

Several were sad as they couldn't stay because of other commitments, but seven of the women joined Abigail to accomplish the sweet mission she believed God had sent her on.

One of the newest members of Bible Study was from South Africa. Mariette was a delightful woman and entertaining as well, Abigail thought.

Abigail asked her to be in charge of mixing the batter. Mariette quickly gave the red mixer a nickname. From then on, it was known as Red Betty. She and Red Betty mixed batter and frosting with joy.

Each lady had such individual and wonderful talents. Some decorated cupcakes, some folded boxes, and others filled the cupcake tins. But each one did their job with a smile. Their hearts were filled with the love of Jesus.

Abigail watched the buzz going on in the Peace House kitchen. It was a scene she had dreamed of for a long time.

"Thank you, Lord," she whispered.

After the cupcakes were frosted and boxed up, the ladies joined hands and asked God to direct them as they set out to deliver the treats.

Abigail prayed. "We love you, Lord, and we thank you for your precious plans to show love! We want your eyes and compassion and your love to overflow out of each one of us today. In Jesus' precious name, Amen."

The group delivered a box of cupcakes to Lily, the clerk from the grocery store that day, and her daughter, Lexi. The surprised looks on their faces were priceless.

Two boxes of cupcakes went to a classroom full of school children. Mommies signed up to bring treats for the class. The cupcakes hit the spot!

Five dozen went to the Christian School.

Fifteen dozen went home with the Tuesday night girls. Some even took extra boxes to deliver, in hopes of blessing their friends and sharing God's love with them.

One of the ladies, Sandy, was going to the laundromat and decided to take a box of cupcakes and see what God had planned.

She asked God, "What does love require of me today?'"

She listened to God and was obedient. She shared the cupcakes with a mother and her two sweet children.

As she did, she asked the mother how she could pray for her.

The woman was surprised by her question, but she answered without hesitating. "Please pray that I will be a good mother," she said as she began to cry. Sandy hugged the young lady and prayed for her. A new friendship formed because of a surprise cupcake delivery.

It wasn't about the cupcakes at all; it was about taking time in the midst of busyness to ask God a simple question: *what does love require of me today?*

Too often we underestimate the power of a touch, a smile, a kind word, a listening ear, an honest compliment, or the smallest act of caring, all of which have the potential to turn a life around.

—Leo Buscaglia

chapter seven

There was one particular Bible study participant that had captured Abigail's heart, as well as the other ladies in attendance.

Eva was a joy to be around. Petite, with blondhair, she was expecting a baby girl and her stomach looked out of place on her small frame, like a basketball tucked under her shirt. She was going to name her baby Heidi. The women were giddy with excitement as they anticipated the baby's arrival.

Eva had found her place among the women, but more importantly, she had fallen in love with Jesus. She was developing a deep, personal, intimate relationship with her Savior. His presence in her life was apparent in all she did and said. Abigail noticed that the other women seemed envious of this young woman's spiritual growth and enthusiasm for the Lord.

Eva had knocked on the door of the Peace House one day, very pregnant and with nowhere to go. She had heard this was a place where girls could get help, so they invited her into the house and into their hearts. Eva had been staying at the Peace House along with Ruthie and Mrs. White.

The bond between the three had grown deep in just a few short weeks. Ruthie and Eva did most of the housework and cooking while Mrs. White did the bookkeeping and ran the business side of Peace House Ministries. They planned and prepared meals together and enjoyed sharing good food and conversation. Trying new recipes was quite entertaining, and they had found several they wanted to prepare for the first weekend retreat, which was just around the corner. They just knew the ladies attending the retreat would get a kick out of Ziploc omelets.

They decided to give the omelets a test run one morning. They cracked two eggs into a quart-sized freezer bag. They shook it up and added all their favorite ingredients—cheese, ham, mushrooms, and spinach. They sealed the baggie and dropped it into a pot of boiling water and watched as their breakfast was cooked to perfection.

"This will be such a fun treat for the girls at the retreat," Mrs. White said.

"They will love it," Eva said. "It's always fun to try new things."

"Eva, you're like a sponge, so thirsty for knowledge," Ruthie said. "I pray I never teach you anything God would not want me to share."

"You've taught me so much, Ruthie," Eva said as she hugged her new friend. "I will always be grateful for the things you've taught me."

"The Word talks about that," Ruthie continued. "Teachers will be judged more harshly. That keeps me on my knees. But it's still a huge blessing to speak life into you, precious girl."

"Okay, I'll clean up this mess," Mrs. White said. "Why don't you two head to the store? I made a list of some of the things we need."

Mrs. White handed a list to Ruthie and Eva, and they headed out on their errand.

Eva had grown to love grocery shopping. The manager, Dean, was so friendly, and it seemed he had directed his employees to show kindness to every customer, but especially to the pregnant girl. They were always going out of their way to be helpful.

After they finished at the store and put the groceries away, Eva excused herself. "I'm pretty tired," she said. "I think I'll take a nap."

"Rest up," Ruthie said. "This afternoon we can work on the gifts for the retreat ladies."

Once Eva was upstairs, Ruthie went to see what Mrs. White was doing. She found her asleep in her favorite chair with her Bible lying open across her lap.

Ruthie decided she might as well take a nap herself. But shortly after falling asleep, she was jolted awake by Eva's cry for help. She rushed upstairs to find Eva, a look of sheer panic across her face.

"My water broke," she said. "Ruthie, Heidi is coming now!"

"Okay, stay calm," Ruthie said. "I'll tell Mrs. White to get ready."

Ruthie quickly went downstairs. She gently rubbed Mrs. White's shoulder to wake her.

"The baby is coming. We have to get Eva to the hospital," Ruthie told Mrs. White. She could feel the panic rising in her throat.

"It's so sad our hospital doesn't deliver babies," Mrs. White said. "This could be a long ninety-five miles drive to get to the hospital. Lord, help us."

"Let's call Abigail," Ruthie said. "She'll have to drive us. Her car is much more reliable than mine."

Mrs. White could tell Ruthie was getting more nervous by the minute.

"Go get Eva and help her down the stairs," Mrs. White said. "I will call Abigail."

Mrs. White uttered a silent prayer and picked up the phone from the table beside her chair. After a few rings, she heard the familiar voice.

"Abigail, Eva's water just broke. Can you drive us to the hospital? Please come quickly."

"I'll be right there," Abigail said. "I'll call Mimsey on my way and have her meet us at the Peace House."

The four women were tucked into Abigail's SUV. They were determined to make it to the hospital before Heidi decided to make her appearance.

Ruthie sat beside Eva holding her hand. Abigail noticed Ruthie looked more nervous than the young girl about to have a baby.

Mimsey, being the practical one, asked a hundred questions. "Is your Medicaid all set up?" she asked.

Eva nodded her head. The labor pains were starting to get stronger, and she was finding it hard to talk.

Abigail wasn't thinking about Medicaid. She knew all the details would work themselves out. She was excited; it had been a long time since she had experienced the miracle of birth, one of God's greatest miracles.

The friends were doing all they could to keep Eva comfortable during the ninety-five-mile drive. Mrs. White was sitting next to Eva, praying and whispering calming words to her.

She smiled at them between contractions to let them know she was okay. With each mile, Eva's pain grew more intense. The contractions were coming closing together.

Abigail, Ruthie, Mimsey, and Mrs. White prayed the entire way.

"Girls, we are going to have to speed up if we're going to make it to the hospital before this baby comes," Mrs. White said. She spoke as if the sin they were about to commit wouldn't really qualify since God knew their state of emergency.

"Okay, you got it," Abigail said as she stepped on the gas. "Don't stop praying!"

As they sped down the highway, the sun slipped beyond the horizon. Abigail passed a red Mustang, and within minutes, it was passing her. The car had to be going ninety miles per hour.

As they got further down the highway, they saw the red Mustang stop along the side of the road. There was road construction, and the driver had pulled over. The driver was a woman and she was talking on her phone, partially blocking the road.

"She could have caused an accident," Mimsey said. "What is she doing?"

Eva's contractions were coming every minute, and the pain was getting to be unbearable.

"Anyone ever deliver a baby?" Abigail asked.

"No, I watched once, but I'm not sure I could do it," Mrs. White said, looking a little squeamish.

"Well, you may have to," Ruthie said. "I think Heidi is coming."

"How close are we to the hospital?" Mrs. White asked.

"We are still twenty miles out." Mimsey reported.

"Okay, we're pulling over," Abigail announced. "We are going to have to deliver this baby."

The women took Mrs. White's wheel chair out of the back of the SUV and directed Eva to lie down.

"You're going to deliver Heidi right here on the side of the road?" Eva asked as she screamed in pain.

"Yes, I believe we are," Abigail said calmly. "I don't think she's going to give us a choice."

"What should I do?" Mimsey asked.

Just then sirens pierced the night air.

"A police car," Mimsey shouted. "Surely they know how to deliver a baby."

Mimsey flagged the officer down. As he pulled up, he rolled the window down.

"Officer, we are having a baby in the back of this car. Can you help?"

"A baby?" the officer said, looking confused. "Lady, I got a report of a drunken driver, and the person who reported it gave me your tag and vehicle description."

"Sir, nobody is drunk. We were just excited and scared and we were trying to get to the hospital before the baby arrived, but we obviously aren't going to make it. Sorry, we were speeding, but we were just trying to get to the hospital." Mimsey rambled.

"So you aren't drinking and driving?" the officer said.

Mimsey was getting annoyed. "Please tell me you know how to deliver a baby," she urged.

Before he could answer her, the cry of a newborn filled the night.

The police officer and Mimsey ran around to the back of the SUV.

"Heidi is here, and she is beautiful," Abigail exclaimed. "Eva, you did great! Now let's get you to the hospital."

"I'll lead the way," the officer said. "You'll get there faster that way."

Abigail was worried that Eva was losing too much blood. They loaded Mrs. White and were ready to go again.

"Mimsey, please drive," Abigail said. She held Eva's hand and prayed. She didn't know what else to do. She placed the baby on Eva's tummy. The umbilical cord was still attached. She had no idea what to cut the cord with or if she should.

When they arrived at the hospital, the medical staff whisked Eva and Heidi away. Thankfully, the police officer had called ahead.

As Mimsey helped Mrs. White get out of the car and into her wheelchair, she noticed the same red Mustang parked in the hospital parking lot.

The three women waited anxiously in the waiting area. They thanked God for all the miracles he performed to get them to the hospital safely.

Just then, the door opened, and a doctor made her way over to them. Mimsey did a double take. It was the driver of the red Mustang.

She didn't think her friends recognized her. But the doctor recognized Mimsey.

"You're the ladies in the white Expedition, aren't you?"

"Yes," Mimsey said.

"Who delivered the baby girl?" the doctor asked.

"We all did," Mrs. White said quickly.

"You could be sued for practicing without a license," the doctor said. "You had no business delivering a baby along the side of the road. You should have called 911."

The doctor was very short with them. Mimsey didn't appreciate her tone of voice.

"I think God sent a doctor to help, but she just drove away." Mimsey snapped back.

Abigail looked at Mimsey, summoning her to be quiet. "We are so sorry," Abigail said. "It wasn't our plan to deliver a baby. But she was ready to make her appearance, and there was no stopping her. God brought her into this world. We were just there to catch her."

"Who's related to this girl?" the doctor asked.

No one answered.

"How do you know her?"

"She is a dear friend," Mrs. White said. "We just met her a few weeks ago when she joined our ministry, which helps young girls."

"Well, one of you will have to take responsibility for this girl and her child," the doctor challenged. "Are you willing?"

She was looking directly at Mimsey.

"Yes, ma'am, I certainly am."

As the words escaped her mouth, Abigail noticed Mimsey now seemed to have a new sense of value.

A few hours later, a nurse appeared and told them that Eva had been taken to a room with Heidi.

"You're welcome to go see her now," the nurse said.

She's much kinder than the doctor, Mimsey thought to herself.

The three women were like a bunch of ecstatic grand-mothers. They followed the nurse down the hall toward Eva's room.

"Why was the doctor so upset that we had to deliver the baby?" Mimsey asked.

The nurse's face turned pale. In a whisper, she told the women why their story had hit so close to home for the doctor. "The doctor had to deliver a baby along the side the road once, and the baby didn't survive," the nurse explained. "The baby was the doctor's grandchild."

"She should have pulled over to help you," the nurse continued. "But the tragedy happened not long ago. She just couldn't."

The three women stood stunned. They couldn't imagine the pain and grief the doctor was experiencing.

"It wasn't her fault, but the complications that occurred were not something she could have handled outside a hospital," the nurse said.

"Oh man, I feel so bad for snapping at her," Mimsey said. "Will I ever learn to keep my mouth shut?"

Abigail wondered the same thing all the time about her own mouth.

"We all say things we shouldn't," Abigail said as she hugged her very vocal friend.

"I guess all we can do is pray for the doctor," Mimsey said. "That he will heal the pain and help her get through this. After all, he is the Great Physician."

May the God of hope fill you with all joy and peace as you trust in him, so that you may overflow with hope by the power of the Holy Spirit.

—Romans 15:13

chapter eight

The friends walked into the hospital room and were welcomed by Eva's new mommy glow. Wrapped in a pink blanket, snug in her mother's arms, was sweet Heidi.

"She's absolutely gorgeous," Abigail said.

Ruthie, Mimsey, and Mrs. White nodded in agreement. They all stood around the hospital bed, soaking up the miracle before them.

"You all are the best thing that has ever happened to me," Eva said as she cradled her daughter. "I didn't know God's amazing love for me until I experienced the love that flows from your hearts. Thank you will never be enough."

Abigail squeezed Eva's shoulder and smiled.

"You're a blessing," she said. "It is his love within us that overflows onto you. We're just humbled to get to be a part of his plan."

The tears flowed freely among friends.

"You're stuck with us," Mimsey said. "Heidi can have four grandmas."

Eva nodded her approval as she looked into her daughter's eyes.

"This is going to be one loved and special little girl," Mrs. White said.

"I think it's time to go shopping," Mimsey said. "Isn't that what grandmothers do best?"

"That's a great idea, Mimsey," Abigail said. "Why don't we gather all the necessities so the house is ready when Eva and Heidi come home."

"I have an idea," Ruthie said. "I'll stay with Eva until she's released. You all go home, do some shopping, and get everything ready for Heidi's homecoming." The women agreed to go home, get some rest, and return to pick up Ruthie with Eva and Heidi when they were released from the hospital.

After several hours of fussing over Heidi, the women hugged good-bye and headed home. There were a lot of preparations to be made for the joyous homecoming that awaited them.

They were waiting to be released from the hospital. Both Eva and Heidi were doing well.

Eva was thankful to have Ruthie there to keep her company. It would have been lonely without her.

Hours before they were set to go home, the doctor, much kinder now, stopped by to speak to Eva.

"Eva, there's something we need to discuss," she said. "Heidi didn't pass her initial newborn hearing screening."

"What does that mean?" Eva asked.

Ruthie stood up and went to stand next to her friend.

"Heidi isn't responding to sound," the doctor said. "There is a chance she could have a hearing problem."

"What do we do?" Eva asked.

She had turned pale and worry was evident on her face.

"We will do another hearing screening to see if we get the same results," the doctor said. "We'd like to do that before we release you to go home."

"Okay," Eva said. "Whatever we need to do."

She cuddled Heidi in her arms and whispered words of adoration. The doctor excused herself and left. Ruthie hugged Eva and stroked Heidi's soft cheek.

"It will be okay," Ruthie said. "Why don't I call Abigail and let her know what's going on."

"That's a good idea," Eva said.

Ruthie picked up the hospital phone and dialed Abigail's number. After a few rings, she answered. Ruthie got straight to the point. "Abigail, I think you need to head back to the hospital," Ruthie said. "The doctor just stopped by to tell us that Heidi didn't pass her hearing test. They want to test her again, but they are pretty certain that she can't hear."

"We will be there as soon as possible," Abigail said. "I'll pick Mimsey up, and we will head that way. Will you call Mrs. White and ask her to pray? Have her put Eva and Heidi on the church prayer chain."

"I will call her," Ruthie said.

"Ruthie, you are doing great," Abigail said. "Thank you for calling. Just keep Eva calm, and pray. We will be praying, too. None of this is a surprise to God."

Abigail hung up with Ruthie and immediately called Mimsey. "Get ready. We have to head back to the hospital," Abigail said. "The doctor thinks Heidi has a hearing problem."

As Abigail spoke the words, fear paralyzed her.

"I'll be ready," Mimsey said. She hung up without saying good-bye.

Abigail and Mimsey prayed the entire way to the hospital. They knew it was the best way to support Eva as she waited for the results of the second hearing test. The drive seemed so long, but they did not stop.

When they finally arrived at the hospital, they found Eva holding Heidi, just as she had been the night she was born. Her face was pale. Worry consumed her. Ruthie sat with her arms around her trying to comfort her amidst so much uncertainty.

Questions raced through Abigail's mind. She knew she wasn't the only one with questions. As she looked at the beautiful baby, God's creation, she wondered how something could be wrong with something so tiny and so perfect. She knew deep down that God didn't make mistakes.

Ruthie finally broke the silence.

"No one knows why things like this happen," Ruthie said. "We serve an awesome God, and he has a plan we may not understand, but we can pray and ask for his help through it all."

Eva began to cry. The women gathered around her and tried to offer words of comfort.

It wasn't long before the doctor returned with another doctor, an audiologist. The doctors informed everyone that the test was conclusive, and Heidi was indeed deaf.

"Because we've discovered this so early, Heidi will no doubt flourish," the audiologist said.

Those were the words Eva needed to hear. She felt a spark of hope.

"An implant would allow Heidi to hear," the audiologist said. "Without insurance, however, we aren't sure she would qualify for the procedure."

As the doctors continued to talk about the pros and cons of an implant, Mimsey felt a familiar tug at her heart.

God was trying to get her attention.

The more the doctors spoke, the more she looked at Eva and her baby girl. Mimsey knew what the Lord was asking her to do.

She felt it in her spirit. He was telling her, "This is my plan for you."

She was supposed to take Eva and Heidi under her wing. She was supposed to bear the financial burden of the surgery and help meet their daily needs.

After the doctors left the room, Mimsey shared what she felt God was asking her to do.

"What do you mean?" Eva asked.

"I've talked to my husband and we agree that you and Heidi should come live with us," Mimsey said. "We can give you both all you need financially, spiritually, emotionally, and physically."

"But what about your business?" Eva asked. "Taking us in is a huge responsibility."

"I've felt for quite some time that God has been asking me to sell my insurance agency. He keeps telling me he has more for me, something of more eternal value. This arrangement would be the joy of my life."

Mimsey couldn't believe what she was saying. Was she finally stepping out in faith and saying yes to God? Was he moving, or was she just trying to take matters into her own hands like she had done so many times before?

Something about this was different. There was no fear. No uncertainties. She had complete peace. It had to be God.

She looked at this young mommy and her precious baby and knew they were meant to be a part of her family.

She soaked up the moment.

"You would do that for us?" Eva asked.

"Yes, I love you so much, and I love Heidi too. I want the best for you and God has put you right under my nose so that I wouldn't miss this great opportunity."

"I don't want to be a burden," Eva said.

"We have plenty of room," Mimsey said. "The two rooms at the other end of our home are empty. They need life, and you two are the life they need."

Eva nodded as tears rolled down her face.

"We would love that," she said.

Eva was bursting with joy as she left the hospital. Knowing she was going home, to a family who loved her and her daughter, made the challenges she faced seem weightless. As the weeks went by, Mimsey, Eva, and Heidi adjusted to their new living situation.

Heidi was a sweet baby. She was eating and sleeping and thriving. The doctors felt she would be ready to receive an implant by the age of three.

The audiologist encouraged Eva and Mimsey to learn sign language in order to communicate with Heidi until she had the surgery.

Mimsey and Eva worked at it daily, and the little girl blossomed.

Something about it seemed strange, but they both felt they should read to Heidi, even though she couldn't hear them.

They were captivated at how she watched their lips move. She smiled and giggled in response to them. They read the Bible to her daily, as well as their favorite children's books. They told her stories and made sure she knew how much she was loved by so many. They visited the Peace House often and all the women were overcome with love for the little girl.

Eva began attending school to finish her high school education. Mimsey was delighted to care for Heidi when her mommy was at school, in a Bible study, or working on homework. Mimsey sometimes wished Eva would ask to go out with friends so that she could get a break, but she took her job as mommy seriously. She knew it was her first priority.

Eva was still going to church and Bible study. God was doing big things in her life. He had given her a hunger and thirst for him that she couldn't quench. She never missed her quiet time with the Lord. Sometimes it just happened later in the day when Heidi was cooperating.

She was determined to graduate so she could support her little girl. Every day she prayed to be a Godly mother and woman. She spent hours praying for her daughter.

During a study called "Praying Circles Around Your Children" by Mark Batterson, Eva had learned to choose scriptures to pray for Heidi. In her journal, she had written Heidi's name and circled it. Out to the sides, she wrote all her prayers for her daughter. Her list was long, but God was faithful. She prayed Jeremiah 29:11–14. She knew he had plans for her sweet baby girl; she was special to him. Eva knew the love the Lord had for her baby.

She also prayed a verse from the book of Esther, one of her favorite women from the Bible. She prayed Heidi would be "for such a time as this." She also prayed Isaiah 40:31, that Heidi would wait upon the Lord and mount on wings like eagles.

Many are the plans in a man's heart, but it is the Lord's purpose that prevails.

—Proverbs 19:21

chapter nine

The Darling Diner was buzzing. Lisa, the owner, was busy baking and preparing for lunch. It was Wednesday, and chicken soup was the special. It was the special choice among residents and out-of-town guests. They looked forward to the warm soup and the encouragement that came with each serving, through the Chicken Soup stories.

Abigail was looking forward to a steaming hot bowl. It always warmed her soul. Lisa was catering the retreat, which meant the ladies attending would be in for a treat. Everything Lisa cooked was made with love.

"Hey, Abi," Lisa said as she waved to her friend. "I have something I'd like to ask you about the retreat."

"Great," Abigail said as she slid into a booth. Lisa sat down across from her.

"There's someone who I think should attend," Lisa said with a concerned look on her face. "I just can't get her off my mind."

Abigail looked at her friend with compassion.

"If God is putting someone on your heart, then we will make room," Abigail said. "His will, not ours, is always my motto."

"How many are signed up to attend?" Lisa asked.

"We have six so far. When do you need the final count for food?"

"No rush," Lisa said. "The dishes we're preparing can easily be doubled."

"Oh good, that puts my mind at ease. Twelve of the girls have finished their study, but the house only has room for nine guests. But we will make room. Why don't you invite your friend and come along too?"

"I would absolutely love that," Lisa said. "I can provide the physical food and help serve the spiritual food too."

Lisa was a great friend and sister in Christ. Abigail was excited that she would be attending the retreat with her friend.

"Well, now that that's settled, what can I get you today, and how can I pray for you?" Lisa asked with a warm smile.

"The chicken noodle soup of course, with a scoop of mashed potatoes, and a piece of that amazing strawberry rhubarb pie," Abigail said. She ordered the same thing every week.

"Water to drink?" Lisa asked.

"Yes, please."

"Okay, what's on your heart?"

"Please pray that God will bring exactly who he wants to this retreat and that he will do exactly what he wants to do there. I just want to be his hands and feet and voice." Tears filled Abigail's eyes. She was overcome with emotion at the thought of God's plan for the retreat and the ladies who would attend.

Lisa placed the order pad on the table and took her friend's hands in hers. She prayed for the requests that were on her friend's heart. Abigail hugged Lisa after she prayed and enjoyed a few quiet moments while she waited for her soup.

She thanked the Lord for bringing Lisa and the other women from the diner into her life. It was such a peaceful place. She picked up the special treat waiting for her next to her utensils. She unfolded the piece of paper, and began to read her daily story from the *Chicken Soup for the Soul* books.

As always, it spoke directly to her heart.

> Love is a wonderful thing. You never have to take it away from one person to give it to another. There's always more than enough to go around.
>
> —Pamela J. deRoy

> Lisa, my two-year-old daughter, and I were walking down the street. Smiling down at Lisa, one of them said, "Do you know you are a beautiful little girl?"
>
> Sighing and putting her hand on her hip, Lisa replied in a boring voice, "Yes, I know!"

A bit embarrassed by my daughter's seeming conceitedness, I apologized to the two ladies and we continued our walk home. All the way there, I was trying to determine how I was going to handle this situation.

After we went into the house, I sat down and stood Lisa in front of me. I gently said, "Lisa, when those two ladies spoke to you, they were talking about how pretty you are on the outside. It's true you are pretty on the outside. That's how God made you. But a person needs to be beautiful on the inside, too." As she looked at me uncomprehendingly, I continued.

"Do you want to know how a person is beautiful on the inside?" She nodded solemnly. "Okay. Being beautiful on the inside is a choice you make, honey, to be good to your parents, a good sister to your brother, and a good friend to the children you play with. You have to care about other people, honey. You need to be caring and loving when someone is in trouble or gets hurt and needs a friend. When you do all those things, you are beautiful on the inside. Do you understand what I'm saying?"

"Yes, Mommy. I'm sorry I didn't know that," she replied. Hugging her, I told her I loved her and that I didn't want her to forget what I'd said. The subject never came up again.

Nearly two years later, we moved from the city to the country and enrolled Lisa in a preschool program. In her class was a little girl named Jeanna, whose mother had died. The child's father had recently married a woman who was energetic, warm, and spontaneous. It was readily apparent that she and Jeanna had a wonderful, loving relationship.

One day, Lisa asked if Jeanna could come over to play for an afternoon, so I made arrangements with her stepmother to take Jeanna home with us the next day after the morning session.

As we were leaving the parking lot, the following day Jeanna said, "Can we go see my mommy?"

I knew her stepmother was working, so I said cheerfully. "Sure, do you know how to get there?' Jeanna said that she did, and following her directions, I soon found myself driving on the gravel road into the cemetery.

My first response was one of alarm as I thought of the possible negative reaction of Jeanna's parents when they learned what had happened. However, it was obvious that visiting her mother's grave was very important to her, something she needed to do, and she was trusting me to take her there. Refusing would send her a message that it was wrong of her to want to go there.

Outwardly calm, as though I'd known this was where we were going all along, I asked, "Jeanna, do you know where your mother's grave is?"

"I know about where it is," she responded.

I parked on the road in the area she indicated, and we looked around until I found a grave with her mother's name on the small marker.

The two little girls sat down on one side of the grave, and I sat on the other, and Jeanna started talking about how things had been at home in the months leading up to her mother's death, as well as what had happened on the day she died. She spoke for some time, and all the while Lisa, with tears streaming down her face, had her arms around Jeanna and, patting her gently, said quietly over and over, "Oh, Jeanna, I'm so sorry. I'm so sorry your mother died."

Finally, Jeanna looked at me and said, "You know, I still love my mommy, and I love my new mommy too."

Deep in my heart, I knew that this was the reason she'd asked to come here. Smiling down at her, I said reassuringly, "You know, Jeanna, that's the wonderful thing about love. You never have to take it away from one person to give it to another. There's always more than enough to go around. It's kind of like a giant rubber band that stretches to surround all the people you care about." I continued, "It's perfectly fine and right for you to love both your mothers. I'm sure your own mother is very glad that you have a new mommy to love you and take care of you and your sisters."

Smiling back at me, she appeared satisfied with my response. We sat quietly for a few moments, and then we all stood up, brushed ourselves off, and went home. The girls played happily after lunch until Jeanna's stepmother came to pick her up.

Briefly, without going into a lot of detail, I told her what had occurred that afternoon and why I'd handled things as I had. To my profound relief, she was very understanding and appreciative.

After they left, I picked Lisa up in my arms, sat down on the kitchen chair, kissed her cheek, and hugged her tightly. "Lisa, I'm so proud of you. You were such a wonderful friend to Jeanna this afternoon. I know it meant a lot to her that you so understood and that you cared so much and felt her sadness."

A pair of lovely dark-brown eyes looked very seriously into mine as my daughter added, "Mommy, was I beautiful on the inside?"[1]

Abigail smiled as she finished reading the story. The Lisa in the story reminded her of her friend Lisa. She was beautiful inside and out.

"Here you go," Lisa said. She sat the warm bowl of soup in front of Abigail. As Abigail sipped the warm broth, she prayed for the girls who would attend the retreat. She had fallen in love with each of them. They were like her daughters. She loved their children, too. She and Adam were like grandparents to them. Their home was always filled with squeals of joy and laughter.

Abigail was blessed to have a husband who understood her heart for women. He was so supportive of the work God had called her to do and welcomed each woman into their home. He was the only good male role model many of them had ever had.

She hoped the Holy Spirit would continue to stir within them and they would be set free from the sin that entangled them, just as he had done for her.

Through the study, Abigail prayed they would become Healed Helpers. She wanted them to be in tune and listen for the calling God had for their lives. Abigail believed many of them were capable of becoming leaders in the Peace House. Maybe they would desire to lead Bible studies. Someday maybe one of them would take her place at this amazing house that God had given and follow the path she and Mrs. White had dreamt of most of their lives.

Peace I leave with you; my peace I give you. I do not give to you as the world gives. Do not let your hearts be troubled and do not be afraid.

—John 14:27

chapter ten

Abigail was busy. She was wrapping up a final design job before closing Abigail Kurtain's Interior Design shop.

It was bittersweet. She loved design, but she knew God was calling her to focus on her family and the Peace House.

She had been working on the home of the Hatler family. Two years ago, they had lost their home and all their belongings in a fire. The fire had started on Christmas morning. A fire in the fireplace had caused the tragedy. They rebuilt on the same lot, and Abigail had been asked to decorate the new home. Abigail and Susan had become good friends through the design process. The Hatlers had four children, and God had shown himself faithful to them throughout the trials they had endured.

As Susan chose new items for her home, it became a privilege for Abigail to pray for her and the new home. She prayed the home would feel even more peaceful than it had before the fire and that the children would feel safe. As Abigail prayed for Susan and her family, she felt God tugging on her heart, asking her to invite Susan to the retreat. She had been through so much loss, and healing was needed. The retreat would be the perfect place for healing to begin.

Abigail decided to extend an invitation to Susan that afternoon.

Susan arrived later that afternoon to look over fabric swatches. She was trying to choose the perfect pattern and colors for the drapes in the formal dining room.

Abigail made a pot of tea and put a platter of cookies on the table. She brought up the retreat as the two women flipped through fabric swatches.

"Susan, do you know about the ministry God has placed on my heart?" Abigail asked.

"I know you help hurting women," Susan said. "That God brings them to you and shows you what to do, and you do it. I admire what you do and hope to join you someday. Maybe once this home is finished and my kids are a bit older."

"We would love for you to join us at the Peace House," Abigail said.

"Do you have a young mother with children who could use some help right now?" Susan asked. "You know my heart is for kids. I'd love to help with whatever they need."

Susan is so kind, Abigail thought. Her passion for helping kids was evident by the way her face glowed when she talked about it.

"There is always someone who needs help; but right now, God has placed you on my heart," Abigail said.

"Oh me? For goodness sakes, I'm fine," Susan said.

"Well, as I prayed for you this morning, God put your name on my list of people to invite to our very first women's retreat this weekend," Abigail said. "I know you know the Lord and have a deep relationship with Jesus, but you've been through so much these past two years. I think the retreat would be a great time of rest and rejuvenation for you." Abigail explained that the retreat wasn't just for those deep in the midst of trouble and pain, but also for anyone who just needed quiet time to rest in Him.

"If God told you to invite me, then I had better think about it," Susan said. "I will ask my husband and get back to you. I don't think we have any ballgames this weekend, which is a miracle in itself."

Abigail laughed. "There's a spot if you want it," Abigail said.

"Just go ahead and count me in!" Susan said. "I will make it work."

After Abigail and Susan had chosen the perfect fabric for the drapes, they exchanged hugs and said good-bye.

"Abigail, I appreciate you so much. Thank you for all you have done for me," Susan said.

Abigail smiled as Susan closed the door behind her.

There were only a few days left to prepare for the retreat. Abigail had a list of things that she needed to accomplish. There were several items she needed that couldn't be found in their small town, so she decided a trip to the city was in order. She would shop and stop by the hospital to visit her father-in-law. Adam had been in the city with his father all week.

It would take her several hours to get to the city, but she had plenty of worship music and Bible tapes to listen to during the drive. She was eager for the alone time with her Heavenly Father.

After a few hours, she was in need of gas and a clean restroom. Thankfully, she had driven the route many times and knew where the clean restrooms were. Her favorite spot was just around the corner. As she pulled into the parking area, she noticed they weren't as busy as they usually were.

She said good morning to the attendant who was filling the windshield wash buckets.

"I'll be right in to help you," the girl said.

Abigail smiled. "No rush; I only need the restroom," she said.

The store looked empty; but as she walked toward the restroom, she noticed someone coming out of the men's restroom.

She froze. The man walking toward her was her old boyfriend, the father of the child they had decided to abort. He stood directly in front of her. She didn't know what to say.

Thankfully, he spoke first. "Abigail, it's good to see you," he said. "You're looking good."

She struggled to speak.

"Thank you, so do you," she said, her voice barely a whisper.

"It's great I ran into you," he said. "You've been on my mind lately. I've been wanting to talk to you."

"I'm on my way to the city to help my husband Adam with his dad. He's in the hospital." Abigail interrupted. She wanted him to know she was married.

"Yes, I've kept track of you over the years," he said. "You've had a tough go of it, haven't you?" His voice held compassion, which surprised Abigail.

"I've endured some hard times; but thankfully, I serve a loving God who has forgiven me of so much."

He nodded his head. "I would like to ask for your forgiveness," he said. "Will you please forgive me for my part in the abortion of our child?"

She leaned closer to him. She could barely hear the words he spoke.

"I've received the same forgiveness through Jesus Christ and would like to ask for your forgiveness as well," she said. "I forgive you. Will you forgive me?"

He nodded.

In that moment she was flooded with peace and joy, knowing he had given his life to the Lord. She was amazed at the story playing out before her.

"I forgive you," she said.

"I hope you and Adam are happy and pray that God will bless you and your family."

After he said the words, he turned and walked toward the door, leaving Abigail speechless.

She stood in a daze for a moment taking in all that had just happened. She went to the restroom.

As Abigail got back on the road, she couldn't hold back the tears. She wept as she thought of what had just happened. She wept for her unborn child. She wept over God's goodness. She wept because she was forgiven. Years later, she had finally received the final piece of forgiveness that she had longed for.

May the words of my mouth and the meditations of my heart be pleasing in Your sight O Lord, my Rock and my Redeemer.

—Psalm 19:14

chapter eleven

Eva was excited about the upcoming retreat at the Peace House. Mimsey was gracious and had offered to keep Heidi overnight so that Eva could attend.

The Healing for Damaged Emotions study that she had been working on for twelve weeks was difficult, but she knew there would be great rewards for her at the end.

The thought of taking all the pain she had gone through—the terrible abuse and trauma she had endured—and using it for God intimidated and thrilled her at the same time. God was turning what Satan had intended to use for evil into something good.

For God to even allow her to help someone else was mind-blowing and exciting all at the same time.

The day Abigail had been waiting for was almost here. The Peace House would be filled with women near and dear to her.

It was December, and the weatherman warned of below zero temperatures and high snow totals for the weekend.

Abigail was excited at the thought of being snowed in at the Peace House. There was plenty of food, and there would be plenty of great company in the warm house.

No one would bother them as they spent precious time with the Lord. He had plans for the weekend, and no earthly thing would stop it.

Abigail often wondered if the weather guys knew how great her God was. There had been many occasions when the weathermen had been wrong, but not this time. The snow was falling and accumulating fast.

Abigail, Mrs. White, and Ruthie had prayed since the planning stages of the event for God to bring exactly who needed to be there. Abigail was saddened that the weather would keep one of the girls from attending. Paula had to drive from the city, and there was just no way she could make it on the slick and snow-covered roads.

Abigail hated that she would miss the retreat, but she would rather Paula would stay off the hazardous roads and remain safe. There was no reason to risk it. There would be other retreats. She prayed this would be the first of many. The other girls were excited and if they were honest, one reason was because they would get a child-free weekend.

"I don't even get to go to the bathroom by myself," one of the girls had told Abigail. "This will be an awesome and great quality time with the Lord. It doesn't get much better than this."

Abigail was thankful for the church women who had stepped up to babysit for those who didn't have childcare arrangements.

With Paula unable to attend, Abigail began to pray and ask God who he wanted to fill the vacant spot.

The Peace House could accommodate nine ladies. So far the girls from Bible study would fill all but one bed. The additional guest was being prayed for; God knew who would be there. Abigail knew God would meet each woman exactly where she needed him most. She couldn't wait to see the God moments that were in store.

The house was buzzing with last-minute preparations. Praise and worship resonated throughout the house.

Lisa was busy preparing the food. The smell of the desserts baking in the oven made Abigail's stomach rumble. Mrs. White was working on the notebook that each girl would receive, including an itinerary of the weekend. Abigail hoped it would be a notebook they would cherish and take home with them—a small reminder of their time at the Peace House and the special weekend they had.

Ruthie cleaned and prayed over every square inch of the house. She loved being in charge of this task. She was nervous about sharing her story with the attendees. She prayed and busied herself with cleaning to take her mind off her nerves. She asked God to give her peace.

Abigail was putting the finishing touches on the gift bags the girls would receive, while singing along to her favorite worship music. She loved how the bags had turned out. The brown paper sacks were filled with colorful tissue paper, and loopy bows of twine adorned them. Each guest would receive a journal, a feather pen, candy, and a bottle of luscious smelling lotion. She placed a gift bag on each bed and prayed for the girl who would sleep there. About the time Abigail finished placing the gift bags on beds, she heard Ruthie scream. She raced down stairs and found Ruthie in the basement. Water was falling from the ceiling.

"What's going on?" Abigail asked.

"That's not just water," Ruthie said. "That's sewer water."

A sewer pipe had burst and sewage was running into the beautifully cleaned craft room.

"What happened?" Mrs. White yelled down toward the others. She was sitting in her wheelchair, unable to get to where the excitement was happening.

"We have a big mess," Abigail said. "A pipe burst and there is dirty water all over the place."

"Oh no, what do you want me to do?" Mrs. White asked.

"Call the plumber Bob! Ask him to come quickly," Abigail shouted. "Ruthie, let's empty that big tote and set it under the pipe to catch what we can to keep it from running all over the floor."

"Bob isn't answering," Mrs. White shouted. "I left a message. He usually calls back pretty quickly."

Mrs. White sat at the top of the stairs and prayed. "Lord, you know what is going to happen right here tonight. In Jesus's name, we cancel the mission that Satan and his demons have over this house and this retreat." About that time the smell hit her. "Girls, get upstairs," Mrs. White shouted. "The smell coming from down there is not healthy."

Abigail and Ruthie did as Mrs. White said.

"We have enough time to get this cleaned up as long as we can get a plumber here soon," Abigail said. "That has to be our prayer. We have to believe that this accident will not postpone our retreat plans, and the Lord knows we need the restrooms to be working."

"The Lord has great things for us this weekend that is why Satan wants to stop it," Mrs. White said. "This is just a hurdle, but we will get over it. Let's pray. You girls get on your knees, please."

Abigail and Ruthie got on their knees before the Lord.

Mrs. White prayed again. "Lord this is your house and your retreat. We ask in Jesus name for your will to be done. We want your will and not ours. Please help us to accomplish what you have for us and allow the Holy Spirit to move among us. We want to be your hands and feet. Lord, you know we need a plumber now. Please provide. In the majestic name of Jesus, we pray all these things. Amen."

Mrs. White smiled as she always did. Abigail knew she very much wanted to get on her knees and hated that she was physically unable.

Just then the phone rang.

"Hello?" Ruthie said.

"Yeah, this is Bob the plumber. I'm sorry, but I'm out of town this weekend. You'll have to find someone else."

"Okay, we will see what we can do," Ruthie said quietly.

"I'll check with you when I get back and make sure everything is okay," Bob said. "We need to redo all those pipes in the basement. We can talk about that next week."

"Thanks for your help," Ruthie said as she hung up the phone.

She looked at Abigail and Mrs. White, "Bob is out of town."

"Maybe Lisa knows someone we can call," Abigail suggested.

Sure enough, she did. Ruthie called immediately.

The receptionist was kind and understanding as Ruthie explained what the problem was and the urgency of the situation.

"I have a service man in the town near you," the receptionist said. "Let me call him and see how close he is to finishing that job. I'll call you right back. I can tell you're desperate to get this fixed. I will do everything I can to help you."

Ruthie hung up and waited for the call back.

"Let's watch God do his thing here," Mrs. White said as she smiled.

They immediately had a peace come over them. God was in control, and he would complete his plan.

The ladies finished the tasks that needed to be completed and didn't require water.

The only thing left to do was clean up the mess in the basement.

It wasn't too long before the plumbing company receptionist called to say the plumbers would be on their way in an hour.

"It's the soonest they can get there," she said.

"That will work," Ruthie said. They would be ready for the retreat in plenty of time.

Amazingly the water at the kitchen sink was working. So the meal preparations continued as planned. The table was beautifully set with a gorgeous black, red, gold, and sage green designer print tablecloth. The napkins were a coordinating fabric. They used gold metallic chargers and crystal goblets and beautiful dishes.

The centerpiece consisted of votive candles surrounded by gold cords, tassels, and cross-shaped confetti. It was low enough that they could still see one another to have conversations.

The table was so inviting it made the ladies smile as they anticipated the meal that would be shared there with new friends. As they admired the table, the doorbell rang.

The plumbers had finally arrived.

Ruthie rushed to answer the door. "Thank you so much for coming to help us." She directed them down to the basement.

They immediately began to repair the broken pipes.

Another plumber showed up to assist. As he walked into the house, he became curious as he noticed the guest book.

The ladies in the kitchen overheard him ask the other guys, "What kind of a place is this that you have to sign in?"

"It's a home for women. It's God's house," one of the plumbers answered. "Don't be asking questions."

It wasn't long before the problem was fixed. One of the workers stepped into the kitchen.

"Can I ask you ladies a question and it's not about the sewer?"

Mrs. White was quick to answer. "Sure."

"Do you think there's a war on Christmas?" the plumber asked.

"Yes, it's a war on Jesus," Mrs. White said. "The world wants Jesus out of the picture and to have him replaced by Santa Claus."

Abigail and Ruthie could tell the plumber liked Mrs. White's answer.

"That's exactly what I told my daughter," he said. "Thank you for verifying that what I told her was right."

With that, the plumbing crew loaded up their tools and left the Peace House.

Mrs. White thought it would have been great to have more time to discuss the plumber's question at length, but they had a mission to accomplish.

The women scurried to clean up the mess left from the broken pipe. They lit candles to mask the odor left from the plumbing mishap. The girls would be arriving in fifteen minutes.

God is faithful, who has called you into fellowship with His son, Jesus Christ our Lord.

—1 Corinthians 1:9

chapter twelve

The doorbell rang signaling the arrival of the first guest.

Ruthie rushed to open the door and was greeted by Eva's vibrant smile.

"I'm so excited about this weekend," Eva said.

"Come in, come in," Ruthie said. "How does it feel to have some time to yourself?"

"Mimsey is such a blessing to keep Heidi so that I can be here," Eva said. "But it's strange not having her with me."

One by one each girl arrived and Ruthie, Mrs. White, and Abigail greeted each of them. Ruthie showed them to their rooms where their gift bags awaited them.

A feeling of peace and the presence of the Holy Spirit filled the house.

After getting settled in their rooms, the girls enjoyed a cup of coffee punch in the kitchen until it was time for dinner. The smell coming from the kitchen was heavenly.

Once everyone had arrived, the girls checked the name cards and found their place at the table.

Abigail noticed everyone seemed to feel welcome and comfortable around the table. Lisa scooped salad onto salad plates and handed them to Abigail. She served each girl. Mrs. White sat at the head of the table and kept the conversation flowing.

After the salad was consumed, the main course was served.

Lisa had prepared deep-dish lasagna with a side of corn and French bread.

As the ladies enjoyed dinner, Mrs. White asked them to take turns introducing themselves and sharing a bit about themselves.

"Let us know why you came to the retreat and what you hope God teaches you this weekend," Mrs. White said.

Abigail realized many of the girls' answers were the same. They wanted more of God in their lives. They wanted to experience his peace and complete healing. They wanted to know how to turn their pain into something God would use to help others.

Abigail had been a counselor to several of them, and they were there because Abigail had listened to God's leading and extended an invitation to them. It brought Abigail joy to see that they were already beginning to relate to one another.

The girls continued to chat as their dinner dishes were cleared from the table and dessert was served. As Lisa brought out the molten lava cake, the girls agreed they were too full to enjoy it.

"We can save it for later," Abigail said. "We can begin our program and take a break for cake later."

"Let's go into the living room, and we will get started," Mrs. White said.

The living room was extremely peaceful, only lit by the warm glow of a lamp. The sweet smell of burning candles was inviting. The girls got comfortable with a blanket and a cup of tea.

Abigail knew tonight would be the final step of healing for many of the girls. If God was asking them to lay anything else at the foot of the cross, she was certain they would know.

Mrs. White began by telling the girls how the Peace House had been a dream of hers for many years.

She shared her testimony, the pain of her past and the loss of her husband in a tragic car accident.

"It's because of an amazing gift from my aunt that I could afford this beautiful home," Mrs. White said.

Then she told them about the box.

How she had filled it with books, letters, money, and pearls and made sure that Ruthie would find it. The girls were in awe of the story. They couldn't believe God's sovereignty and his attention to detail.

"Have any of you seen God work a miracle in your life?" Mrs. White asked the girls.

One of the girls spoke up; her voice was soft, almost a whisper. "My son Isaac has a dog named Diesel. He loves him so much. Diesel got sick and stopped eating and drinking. Isaac prayed and asked God to make Diesel better and to help him get his appetite back. He even told God he would stop eating until God healed his dog. The next morning, Isaac was crying tears of joy. He ran to me shouting, 'Diesel is eating and drinking. God did what I asked, and now I can eat too. God is real, Mom! He really does care about us!"

The girls thanked God for how he had answered the little boy's prayer.

"God loves each of you and has a plan for your life, and it is good," Mrs. White said. She opened her Bible and read Jeremiah 29:11. "For I know the plans I have for you, declares the Lord. Plans to prosper you and not to harm you. Plans to give you hope and a future." Mrs. White flipped from the Old Testament to the book of John. She turned to chapter five and began to read the story of the man who was lame from birth. "He had laid by the pool of Bethesda for thirty-eight years. When Jesus walked by him he asked, 'Do you want to be healed?' I want you to search your hearts and think about that question," Mrs. White said. "If Jesus walked up to you right now and asked you if you wanted to be healed, what would you say? Are you really ready for that?"

The room was silent as the girls pondered the question Mrs. White had asked.

"When God heals, he wants you to pick up the cross and follow him, which requires obedience," Mrs. White continued. "If you obey God, it is going to cost others more than it costs you. That is where the pain begins. If we are in love with our Lord, obedience doesn't cost us anything. It is a delight. But to those who do not love him, our obedience to God costs a lot. It will upset others. They will say to you, 'You call this Christianity?' When our obedience begins to cost others, our human pride is affected. The relationship we have with God should be the same as we have with others. A lack of progress in our spiritual life results when we try to bear all the costs ourselves because it's something we cannot do," Mrs. White said. "We are involved in the purposes of God. If we obey God, he will care for those who have suffered the consequences for our obedience. We must simply obey and leave the consequences with him."

Mrs. White closed her Bible and nodded at Abigail. It was her turn to share how obedience, or lack of, had played a part in her story.

Abigail shared her past choices, her total disobedience, and the incredible pain it had caused her and those around her.

"The cost of disobedience is much higher than the cost of obedience," Abigail said. "I have seen it first hand and believe it with all my heart."

Abigail shared her story, the pain caused by her sin of the abortion. She talked about the prison she locked herself in and the near-death experience she had when she tried to take her life.

"All of these things were because of disobedience to God," she said. "I didn't see it that way at the time, but now I know. I never thought I would tell a living soul about the sins, the terrible sins I have done, but I'm telling you so that you can learn from me."

"Sometimes the pain is still so great, but God has healed my heart and forgiven me of the horrific sin," Abigail said as tears streamed down her face.

Soft music was playing in the background—beautiful, peaceful, almost angelic.

Abigail began to pray. "Holy Spirit, move among us freely and give each of these ladies a complete peace."

The girls were given a mat and a journal and were asked to take them to a quiet place in the house, somewhere they could lay on the mat, like the lame man in the story found in the book of John, and meditate on all they had just heard.

Abigail said, "Ask yourself the question Jesus asked the lame man: do you want to be healed? Are you ready to be obedient and give God 100 percent of your heart? Then when you have had time to think through it, write your answer in your journal. We will gather back in here when we've all completed the exercise."

The ladies had finished the exercise, and it had proven to be a very emotional time. Abigail knew it was the perfect time to enjoy dessert and some light-hearted conversation before moving on to the next phase of the retreat, forgiveness.

After the girls polished off their chocolate cake, they got comfortable and listened to Mrs. White. She told them about the forgiveness she had given and received.

"Forgiveness truly set me free from the agony of self-pity. After I was injured in the car accident that took the life of my sweet husband, I was angry. I lay in bed unable to walk for over a year. Nothing would allow me to walk again, except a miracle of healing that God wasn't doing. I had to get this through my head, that sometimes God doesn't heal us while we are here on earth. One day, as I was thinking about being thankful, God reminded me that I was to be thankful in all things, even being unable to walk. I took a deep breath and thanked him for allowing me to live and be able to use a wheelchair. I even thanked him for giving the idea to the inventor of the wheelchair so I could get around. I was thankful I could use my arms to wheel it around. And I was thankful I could think and pray and read my Bible. My thankful list got very long that day, and I realized I was beginning to feel joy, a joy I had not felt for a very long time. God restored my joy, my faith, and my smile. I was free when I gave it all to Jesus."

Abigail then shared something on forgiveness she had once heard a radio preacher say. "He said, 'You know what

I hate about Christians? When they say, 'I know God has forgiven me, but I just can't forgive myself.' What more do you want? He gave his one and only Son to die for you and that sin. What more do you want him to do?' After I heard those words, I had a total breakthrough," Abigail said. "I finally gave up and accepted what Jesus did for me on the cross. I was free at last!"

Abigail shared how the father of her unborn child had forgiven her. She had forgiven him too. "Men are involved in abortions too," she said. "They hide it just as well as women, but they are dying inside and have probably put themselves into a prison inside their minds. Those men need to find the amazing love and forgiveness Jesus offers them."

After Abigail shared her story, they began a short Bible study called "Ten Steps of Forgiveness." They worked through each step and read each scripture as soft worship music played.

1. Feel the pain, hurt, resentment and hate (Matthew 5:4).

2. Submit yourself to God, recalling how Christ forgave you (Luke 23:33–34; Col. 3:13).

3. Ask for Christ's grace and power to forgive (Luke 11:9–10).

4. Agree to live with the unavoidable consequences of the other person's sins against you (Ephesians 4:31–5:2).

5. Release the offense. Tear up the debt the other person owes you (Matthew 6:12 and The Lord's Prayer).

6. Never bring it up again as a club (Romans 12:17–18).

7. Keep forgiving when your emotions recycle the pain or when the person keeps offending you (Matthew 18:21–22; James 4:7).

8. Reject the sinful act and tolerate it no longer (Romans 12:19–13:5).

9. Turn the vengeance over to God and over to God's human authorities (Romans 12:19–13:5).

10. Replace the old resentful feelings with the forgiving love of Christ (Matthew 12:43–45; Ephesians 4:31–32).

When the last scripture was read, Abigail prayed. "Heavenly Father, I thank you for providing everything I need to forgive others and for my own forgiveness through the atoning death of our Lord Jesus Christ on Calvary's cross. Thank you that what I owe for my sin is paid in full. Right now, bring to my mind the faces or names of anyone whom I need to forgive. With the love and power of the Holy Spirit, I now forgive them. Lead me to reconcile the shattered relationships that are within your will.

"By faith I forgive myself and accept your healing of my emotions, memories, and resentments. I give you full permission to rebuild my self-esteem in the image of our Lord

Jesus Christ. Help me to act out this truth even when my emotions cycle and tempt me to believe the same old lies. Thank you for setting me free. I surrender my life to you. In Jesus's name, amen."

Abigail asked the girls to take the black blindfold they had been given and cover their eyes and sit quietly until they felt they had no un-forgiveness in their hearts.

The music played softly; it was a powerful tool that the Holy Spirit used to free their souls. A rugged cross had been placed at the front of the room; when they felt the freedom from God; they were to lay the blindfold at the foot of the cross. They would exchange it for a white flag of surrender. Once everyone had felt God's presence, together they would sing "I Surrender All."

It was a beautiful picture of a new beginning.

The first day of the retreat was winding down. It was getting late, but not too late for popcorn, sodas, and a movie.

The popcorn became "gourmet" as they added M&Ms, Hot Tamales, and Reese's Pieces to their hot buttered treat.

The movie that had been chosen was called *Loving the Bad Man*. It depicting an incredible display of forgiveness.

The scene in the living room reminded Abigail of a slumber party from her youth. The women were relaxed and having a great time. She could feel the presence of Jesus in the room and believed the women had found true freedom, joy, and peace. It was the perfect way to end an emotional evening.

The next morning the girls gathered in the kitchen for a breakfast surprise.

Ruthie and Mrs. White were excited to teach them how to make Ziploc omelets.

Everyone made an omelet filled with her favorite toppings. They savored their creation over a cup of fresh brewed coffee or tea.

One girl decided to skip breakfast and take advantage of a long, hot shower, something that was rare when you have children. "I haven't had an uninterrupted shower in as long as I can remember," she said.

The girls laughed and encouraged her to enjoy the alone time.

After breakfast it was time to begin the day's lessons. Ruthie would start the morning sessions.

"This is going to be the fun day," she told the girls. "Let's pray before we begin. I have a prayer I would like us to say together."

She handed a sheet of paper to each girl and asked them to join her. They recited the prayer together.

> Dear Heavenly Father, direct my paths by the light of your Word, and instruct me in ways to leave a

clearly marked trail behind for others. I want to use your Word to create environments that will encourage others to flourish. I choose to guard my heart so as not to mistake co-laborers for competitors. Open my eyes to see the fields surrounding my life that are white and ready for harvest. This day I choose to lay aside my right to speak my mind, and I exercise my right to be silent.

After they prayed, Ruthie began. "We want to show you a few ways that might make it easier for you to live in God's presence and to discover God's plan for your life," Ruthie said. "You may be asking, 'Where do we go from here?' 'What does God have in store?' These are questions I heard around the table this morning."

The girls nodded as they listened to Ruthie.

"We don't know what God's plan is until we seek him with all our hearts," she said. "As we read his word, listen to worship music, praise him in song, and spend quality time with him, we will develop a deeper relationship with the God of the Universe, the one who created you."

She grabbed a book and opened it to a bookmarked page. It was *Girls with Swords* by Lisa Bevere. She read from it.

"The sword of God's Word has the Power to sever what entangles us," Ruthie read. "Proverbs 2:12-15 says wisdom will deliver you from the way of evil, from men of perverted speech, who forsake the paths of uprightness to walk in the ways of darkness, who rejoice in doing evil and delight in the perverseness of evil, men whose paths are crooked, and who are devious in their ways." [2]

Ruthie loved God's word more than anything. It was apparent in the way she read his word. His word had saved her life. She hungered and thirsted for the bread of life and prayed the girls would hunger and thirst, too.

"God's word is so very powerful," Ruthie said. "You must read it as often as possible. It will keep you in the presence of God."

Therefore, since we have been justified through faith, we have peace with God through our Lord Jesus Christ.

—Romans 5:1

chapter thirteen

Ruthie had a new love for movies, but not science fiction; however, *The Matrix* had a scene she felt she had to share during the retreat.

She and Abigail had gone to Roswell, New Mexico, for Abigail to speak. The ladies at the church in Roswell had been different than any she had ever worked with before. They were so in love with Jesus; they glowed, similar to how a pregnant woman might look.

Ruthie and Abigail had been amazed at the powerful presence of the Holy Spirit. The women prayed powerful prayers from the depths of their hearts. It had been a life-changing weekend. The Roswell ladies had given Abigail a book, and she had shared it with Ruthie.

The title was *Love Stains* by Bob Johnson. The chapter titled "The Red Pill" had spoken to both of them and was based on a scene from the movie *The Matrix*.

Ruthie started the seven-minute scene, and the girls watched. The two main characters are Morpheus, the one who has seen the truth, and Neo, the one who seeks the truth. Neo could never accept the status quo, and as a result, he found himself in a precarious situation. Then he meets Morpheus, who asks him a simple but life-altering question that involves making a choice between a red pill and a blue one. If Neo chooses the blue pill, his life will continue as is, blissfully blind to reality. However, if he chooses the red pill, he will not be able to turn back from the truth. He will discover the answers that he has been looking for and will experience just how far down the rabbit hole goes. Neo chooses the red pill, and so begins his journey into the unknown.[3]

After they had watched the scene from the movie, Ruthie began to share what was on her heart. "We all face a similar choice in our relationship with God. Will we take the red pill and invite his plans into our lives, without an escape clause? Will we give him full reign over our futures, full permission to prune our lives according to his design? Or would we rather take the blue pill of a comfortable life as usual?"

Ruthie paused and let the girls think about what she had just asked before she continued.

"The choice to give our lives to the Lord is a red pill choice, but after we become believers, we continue to choose the red pill over and over by living a life of surrender," she said. Ruthie held a bowl of red pills (Hot Tamales) and a bowl of blue pills (M&Ms).

"What choice will you make?" she asked.

One by one, each of the girls walked to the front of the room and made her choice.

Ruthie fought back tears as they each chose red over blue.

"You are all in for an exciting life with our Lord," she said. "His plans are for a hope and a future. Many of you have faced hopeless times in your life, but not anymore. We've all tried it our way, and it didn't work out too good, so here we are. Let the God who created you and formed you in your mother's womb have his plan fulfilled. You just gave him permission."

Ruthie was completely out of her element but knew she had to be obedient to the Lord. She asked the girls to repeat a simple prayer.

"Father, take all of me, and do whatever you want with me. I am yours."

They all repeated the words.

"Feels good and kind of scary, doesn't it?" Ruthie asked as she smiled lovingly. "That is how I felt the first time I prayed the prayer. It's like setting off on a grand adventure into the unknown. God took me from roaming the alleys in deep depression to this wonderful place. He is amazing. I have always been exactly where God wanted me to be, and so are you. Once you choose the red pill, the sky is the limit."

Abigail smiled at her friend. She was so proud of the woman God has created Ruthie to be. "Why don't we take a break," Abigail said. "Let's meet back here in ten minutes."

After a short break, the girls opened their copies of *Healing for Damaged Emotions*. It was time to read the final chapter of the study.

The girls had written letters of forgiveness. The letters described all the ugly sins and the pain of their past. Now they would burn the letters and the books to signify the change that occurred during the study and at the retreat.

"Now that we have experienced God's healing power and the amazing forgiveness of Jesus, it's time to lay it at the foot of the cross," Abigail said. "Bundle up and let's meet in the backyard."

It was freezing outside, and snow was falling. The wind was bitter, but it couldn't dampen their spirits. They cleared a place on the ground in front of the big wooden cross that Adam had made for the Peace House.

A giant sign that said Forgive was lying at the base of the cross. The ladies gathered close and huddled under blankets. Abigail lit a fire, and one by one the girls placed their books and letters into the flames. The book burning symbolized letting go of the past. Starting today, they would no longer look back, only forward at all God had for them. Tears flowed freely among the ladies as the significance of the event hit them.

They finally realized that the past was now truly the past. They would never look back and feel the shame and guilt they had prior to this weekend.

One of the girls, a photographer, began to capture the moment with her lens. The flames engulfed the books and letters.

But amidst the smoke and flames, there was an incredible peace.

The girls returned to the house to warm up and enjoy lunch. Lisa had prepared a beautiful salad topped with crispy chicken and a delicious dressing. The lunch conversation turned to all that God had been doing in their hearts since arriving on Friday.

After lunch, they gathered around the fireplace in the living room. The final session of the retreat was about to begin.

Mrs. White started the afternoon with a story about riptides. She handed each girl a bright-colored inner tube similar to the ones they used when they were children.

"You must have your own faith and your own relationship with the Lord," she explained. "You cannot lean on others to get you there. If you were in the ocean and starting to sink, you could hold on to an inner tube, but if someone else didn't have one and grabbed at yours, it could be fatal. The same goes for our faith in Jesus. We can't rely on someone else's faith or their study time or their prayer time. You must put your faith into action and cling to God's Word."

Mrs. White then changed the subject to the importance of healthy friendships.

"Sometimes as women, we have friendships that God never intended for us to have," Mrs. White said. "We must ask God to sever any relationships in our lives that are not from him. If we ask, he will answer. We will survive and eventually thrive."

After Mrs. White finished, the girls took a quick break, while Abigail and Ruthie set up for the closing ceremony.

The table at the end of the living room was covered with a beautiful gold metallic cover. On top of the table lay a thirty-six-inch sword, a gorgeous box with a lid, a white feather pen, and the commitment sheet each lady had signed. In the box were strips of white fabric.

As the girls took their seats one final time, Abigail summed up the weekend and began to share from Ephesians 6. She read verse 17, which described the sword of the Spirit.

"God's Word, when written together, without any spaces spells Godsword," Abigail said. "Isn't that interesting?"

She picked up the book *Girls with Swords* and once again shared a passage by Lisa Bevere. "In 2 Timothy 3:16–17, it says, 'All Scripture is inspired by God and is useful to teach us what is true and to make us realize what is wrong in our lives. It corrects us when we are wrong and teaches us to do what is right. God uses it to prepare and equip his people to do every good work.' This weekend, I pray you have learned that you are all on God's team and each have a job to do. You are to carry the message of the Good News to the world. If you choose to accept this mission, we want you to participate in the closing ceremony. Last night, you traded your black blindfold and replaced it with a white strip of fabric, representing total surrender. Please drape your white strip of fabric over your heart, and then hold the sword and repeat these words:

> "With great endurance, Lord
> I'm going to run this race
> Pressing on toward the goal
> I will follow you with eyes of faith
> Teach me to walk in love
> Shine as a light in me
> Even in the dark
> I will live to be your hands and feet
> Send me, for the glory of your name!"

The girls came one at a time to the front of the room as Abigail, Ruthie, and Mrs. White took turns praying over them. As the girl held a sword, she made a declaration of her willingness to run the race God had for her, and then she signed the bottom of the page. Each of the girls took the pen and signed their names as witnesses. They were ready to surrender all to Jesus. It was a very emotional and powerful ending for the retreat, a weekend filled with the presence of the Holy Spirit. Lives were changed and all by the grace of God and to his glory.

After one final sweet treat, a delicious buttery Bundt cake, the girls were asked to complete an evaluation form so that the next retreat would be better.

As the girls gathered their belongings and hugged goodbye, they promised to go out into the world with anticipation for what God had in store for them.

The house was quiet, all the girls had gone. Abigail, Ruthie, and Mrs. White sat around the table and read the girls' responses.

Abigail went first.

> I love you all so very much. Thank you for not giving up on me. I enjoyed the time we got to spend together at this retreat. I experienced a huge amount of happiness and peace this weekend!"

Then Ruthie shared another.

> I really found this helpful in my walk with Christ. I loved getting to be in his presence and the presence of my new sisters in Christ. I feel this will help a lot to help others in need of healing. Last night was just awesome. I liked the burning of the books and letters and just letting go. This whole experience is just amazing. I'm so thankful for all you did to make this possible. Thank you from the bottom of my heart.

Abigail, Ruthie, and Mrs. White wiped away tears. "I'll read the next one," Mrs. White said.

This weekend was amazing! I had been struggling with forgiving, and now it is done. God revealed himself to me. I did not know what to expect this weekend. I knew I wanted to come hang out with fellow lovers of Jesus.

I also expected to feel the Holy Spirit, to an extent. But I did not expect a complete revelation of him. What I got here this weekend went above and beyond any expectation I could have ever had. I love you all so much. I love Jesus so much. Thank you, Jesus, for this weekend!

Mrs. White took another sheet of paper and began to read.

This was more than I could have ever expected or imagined! I wouldn't have wanted anything to be different. It was perfect!

Abigail took the final piece of paper and shared it with her friends.

I found my "fire" again. I realized it is going to take a lot of work from me, and I am willing! So willing! I needed this time with God and good friends so much more than I knew. You all inspire me so much! Watching you allow God to work through you no matter what it takes…it's amazing! I want to serve our God the way you do! Thank you all so much. The words don't come close to expressing

how thankful I am to have you and Jesus in my life!
The weekend was perfect! I love you!

With tears of joy, the ladies thanked God and soaked up his faithfulness.

For to us a child is born…And He will be called Wonderful Counselor, Mighty God, Everlasting Father, Prince of Peace.

—Isaiah 9:6

chapter fourteen

Mrs. White's health was deteriorating. Physically she was getting weaker, but her spirit was still strong. She continued to greet everyone with a sweet smile and loving words.

Abigail had been sharing some precious moments with Mrs. White. She would sit with her friend and get lost in the conversation. Each visit left Abigail wanting to know more about Mrs. White. God had given her so much wisdom. Abigail couldn't get over how God had allowed their paths to cross.

"Isn't he just the most creative God?" Mrs. White would say with a giggle. She acted like a smitten schoolgirl when she talked about the Lord. She loved him dearly.

Abigail thought of the creativity behind how God had brought Mrs. White into her life. The Holy Spirit had nudged Mrs. White to place the things that were special to her in a box. She had obeyed and filled it with books, pearls, letters, and the money needed to make all her dreams come true. It wasn't a coincidence that Ruthie stumbled across the box and that its contents brought the four women together.

Mrs. White had known her time was short, and it was important for her to find someone to pass the baton to. Abigail had been the perfect recipient. She had the same vision, heart, and compassion for women who needed to be shown the love of God.

When Mrs. White looked at Abigail, she saw the younger version of herself. During their visits, Abigail would ponder about things of the Lord. She had so many questions, and voicing them to Mrs. White always helped Abigail find clarity. Mrs. White's words were worth gold, full of wisdom.

Abigail wasn't the only one to ask deep questions. Mrs. White was always challenging Abigail with her own questions. Stretching her faith. One evening Abigail sat beside Mrs. White in her bedroom. She was too weak to get out of bed and sit in her wheelchair. The bedroom was painted a soft hue of green, and it was peaceful.

Mrs. White wore a pink robe made of silk. She was a picture of heaven sitting up in the bed. Her makeup was perfectly applied; her silver hair curled.

"Would you hand me my Bible?" she asked Abigail.

Abigail reached for the leather bound book sitting on the nightstand. It was worn—a sign of a life devoted to the Lord.

Mrs. White took the Bible and said, "This is my very favorite of all the Bibles I own. I've spent forty years underlining, highlighting, and making notes. I wanted to remember all the ways God had spoken to me through the years."

Abigail wondered what event marked the start of this particular Bible. She would have to ask Mrs. White, but this particular evening, Mrs. White had asked to speak to her.

"How can you cooperate with the Holy Spirit to accomplish the process of renewal in your life?" Mrs. White asked, getting straight to the point.

She didn't give Abigail a single moment to think about her answer. She began teaching, the way Mrs. White was known to do. "You ask God to check you every time you belittle yourself," she said. "When you start doing this, you're in for a surprise. For you may find that your whole lifestyle is a direct or indirect put-down of yourself."

Abigail just listened. She nodded as Mrs. White continued.

"What do you do when someone compliments you? Can you say, 'Thank you, I'm glad you liked that'? 'I appreciate that'? Or do you go into a long song and dance cutting yourself down? Don't ever belittle yourself, Abigail," Mrs. White said sternly.

Abigail felt her cheeks turn red. Mrs. White knew her too well. She could be her own worst critic.

"Abigail, I remember when we first met, you had such a hard time accepting compliments. I'm so happy you have overcome that and you allow the Holy Spirit to renew your mind."

"It's something I have to work on daily," Abigail said. "It's not in my nature to accept compliments."

"This is something you must teach those who have experienced abuse," Mrs. White said. "Abuse leads to this behavior." Mrs. White flipped through the pages of her Bible and pulled out a piece of paper. It was wrinkled and worn. "I want you to make copies of these daily affirmations and give them to those you counsel and study with. I've used these for years. I believe the Lord wants you to use these too."

She handed a small piece of yellowed paper to Abigail.

"I want you to read them out loud to me," Mrs. White said.

Abigail unfolded the piece of paper and began to read slowly. She wanted every word to soak in.

> Lord Jesus, I know you love me. Thank you for making me in an amazing and wonderful way. What you have created is precious. Thank you, Father, for calling me your child. Knowing this gives me a sense of being honored.
>
> God, you declared your value of me when you gave the life of Your Son, Jesus, to redeem me. Thank you for valuing me so highly. Jesus, you have promised to supply all my needs according to your riches. Today I choose to trust you with every need that I have. Thank you for providing for me so fully.
>
> Lord, even before the foundations of the world, you chose to adopt me as your own child. Thank you for having planned for me so carefully. God, thank you for looking at me in Christ and declaring me

accepted and beloved. It is awesome to think that
you are delighted in me.

Abigail sat in silence for a few moments, meditating
on the words. "Mrs. White, this is wonderful and you are
so right. I struggled with being able to take a compliment for so long. I still have to catch myself sometimes
so that I don't belittle myself. Thank you so much for
sharing this."

"I hope it helps you as much as it has helped me throughout the years," Mrs. White said. "It was part of my morning
quiet time with the Lord. I pray it will become part of yours
and those you share it with."

Abigail noticed tears filling Mrs. White's eyes as
she spoke.

"I will cherish these words, and I thank the Lord for
giving them to you and that you shared them with me. I'm
sure I will become a much stronger person after reading
them daily."

Abigail knew the power of God's Word. She knew that
what she chose to meditate on had a direct impact on her
thoughts and the words she spoke.

"Long ago, I learned to pray Psalm 19:14," Abigail
said. "Before speaking to anyone, I ask for guidance: 'May
the words of my mouth and the meditations of my heart
be pleasing in your sight, Lord Jesus, my rock, and my
redeemer.'" She recited the words from heart.

Mrs. White smiled with delight. "I think it's time I get some rest. Thank you for coming by, Abigail. I cherish our times together."

Abigail stood and wrapped her arms around her friend. "I love you, Mrs. White, more than you'll ever know."

"I love you too," Mrs. White said.

As Abigail drove home that night, she thanked God for showing her his love through such a beautiful woman, friend, and mentor. She thought of the worn piece of paper Mrs. White had given her, tucked inside her pocket.

Mrs. White had carried that piece of paper in her Bible for so many years. It was similar to the worn note that Abigail carried in her own Bible. Her pastor had given it to her while she was in the mental hospital.

Written on it were these words:

> I am deeply loved, totally forgiven, fully pleasing, accepted and complete in Christ.

She read the words often to remind her of where she had been in her life and how very far God had brought her.

As the weeks went by, Mrs. White's health grew worse. Abigail spent as much time as she could with her friend.

She knew Mrs. White's time on earth was short. It wouldn't be long until she met her Savior face-to-face.

It was hard for Abigail to be sad because she knew heaven was the place Mrs. White yearned for. She wanted to be with Jesus. Abigail had peace, but she was going to miss her friend terribly. She would leave a legacy that would continue for a very long time.

Abigail, Ruthie, and Mimsey would make sure every lady who entered the Peace House knew the dream that had been Mrs. White's for so long—a dream that had finally become reality.

Tonight was going to be a very special time. The thought of sitting beside this woman who prayed so earnestly for wisdom from God gave Abigail butterflies.

When she arrived at the Peace House, Ruthie greeted her.

"Mrs. White seems especially at peace tonight," Ruthie said. "She knew you were coming. She spent the day telling me stories about her past. I have learned things I didn't know about her. I'll have to share them with you sometime."

Abigail noticed Ruthie seemed to have an extra sweet presence of God on her face.

"Okay, I want to hear it all. I love you, Ruthie, and thank you for all you do for Mrs. White. She loves you so much."

Abigail hugged Ruthie, who had finally learned to enjoy the sweet embrace of a fellow sister in Christ.

Ruthie smiled as she watched Abigail walk toward Mrs. White's room.

The room seemed more beautiful than usual and had a fragrance so sweet that she felt the presence of the Lord the moment she entered.

Mrs. White's eyes were closed, so she sat down quietly in the chair beside the bed. Abigail prayed and asked God to give her the right words to comfort Mrs. White and for the Holy Spirit to comfort her in the moment. As she finished her prayer, Mrs. White opened her eyes and smiled the sweet smile Abigail had grown accustomed to.

"Good evening, Abigail. Thank you for coming to visit this evening."

"I would not have missed it, Mrs. White."

"I have some very important things to talk to you about, and God has shown me that I must say these things to you tonight," Mrs. White said. "I have put off talking about your precious grandson's suicide because it causes you so much pain. But God wants you to know something about suicide and his love."

Mrs. White paused and took a deep breath.

Abigail moved to the edge of her seat, not wanting to miss a single word Mrs. White was about to say.

"I know that some people really have hurt you when they asked you if you thought Nick was in heaven," Mrs. White said as she took Abigail's hand. "We both know that Nick loved Jesus with all his heart and just made a terribly wrong choice that day. But God forgives us. That is why he sent his Son to die for us. Jesus died for that sin that day. Nick is in heaven. I believe it, and I know you do too."

Abigail wiped away the tears that were falling freely. Oh, how she wanted everyone to know that she would embrace her grandson in heaven and spend eternity with him, but the devil is good at planting seeds of doubt.

"I want to give you another Bible," Mrs. White said. "It is fairly new to me. It's called The Evidence Bible." She pointed to a Bible on her dressing table, and Abigail stood to get it. She handed it to Mrs. White, who opened it to a page she had marked with a bookmark.

"This Bible has questions that people have asked the author. 'Does someone go to hell for committing suicide?' It is at the top of this page. It caught my attention. This is what it says:

> Those who are adamant that a person who takes his life is committing a mortal sin, and will go to hell, are basing their belief on church doctrine rather than on the Bible. Scripture is silent on the subject. There are no verses that say he who takes his own life shall be damned. According to Scripture, only one sin does not have forgiveness, and that is blasphemy of the Holy Spirit. That means there is forgiveness for every other sin. God forbid that we add to the pain of someone who has lost a loved one through the tragedy of suicide, by making a judgment about their eternal destiny. God is the ultimate Judge, and we should therefore leave the issue in his hands. It

would be wise to follow the biblical example and
not come to any verdict in the case of suicide.

Mrs. White laid the Bible on her lap and looked at
Abigail whose face was wet with tears.

"Abigail, you remember how Nick and his friends were
very sincere that day in your kitchen when they asked
Jesus to be the Lord of their life. After that day, Nick
was different. He loved Jesus with all his heart. That, my
dear, is what makes the difference." Mrs. White paused
before continuing.

She recited Romans 6:14 from memory. "'For sin shall
not be your master, because you are not under the law, but
under grace.' God's grace is what assures you and me of our
eternal destination. I am so thankful for his amazing grace."

Abigail shook her head. Words wouldn't come.

"Abigail, my very favorite song is 'Amazing Grace.' You
know that, don't you?"

"Yes," Abigail whispered. She knew where the conversation was heading.

"I'd like very much for it to be sung at my funeral," Mrs.
White said. "While I'm on that subject, I have a funeral
plan in my top dresser drawer. Please follow my instructions. They are my wishes. I know I can count on you to
follow through with them. Before you go, I have one last
thing to say."

"I'm listening," Abigail said.

"I know the horrible pain in your heart for the loss of your precious grandson. God knows that pain, and he will continue to comfort you with the presence of the Holy Spirit. Keep being the hands and feet of Jesus. I believe you will see your grandson, waiting at the gates of heaven when you arrive. I was not able to meet him while here on this earth, but I believe I will know him in heaven because of my love for his grandma. He will be there when I see Jesus face-to-face."

A smile spread across her face, and she closed her eyes.

She was on her way to meet Jesus.

The funeral was exactly as Mrs. White had requested: a simple graveside service. All that was said about her was that she loved the Lord God with all of her heart, soul, mind, and strength and loved her neighbor the same.

The music said it all. "Give Me Jesus" and "Amazing Grace."

> Amazing Grace, how sweet the sound
> That saved a wretch like me.
> I once was lost but now am found,
> Was blind, but now I see.

The End

notes

1. Canfield, Jack, and Mark Victor Hansen. *A 4th Course of Chicken Soup for the Soul: More Stories to Open the Heart.* Cos Cob, Connecticut: Backlist LLC, 2012.
2. Bevere, Lisa. *Girls With Swords: How to Carry Your Cross Like a Hero* . Colorado Springs: Waterbrook Press, 2013.
3. Johnson, Bob. *Love Stains.* Redding, California: Red Arrow Publishing, 2013.